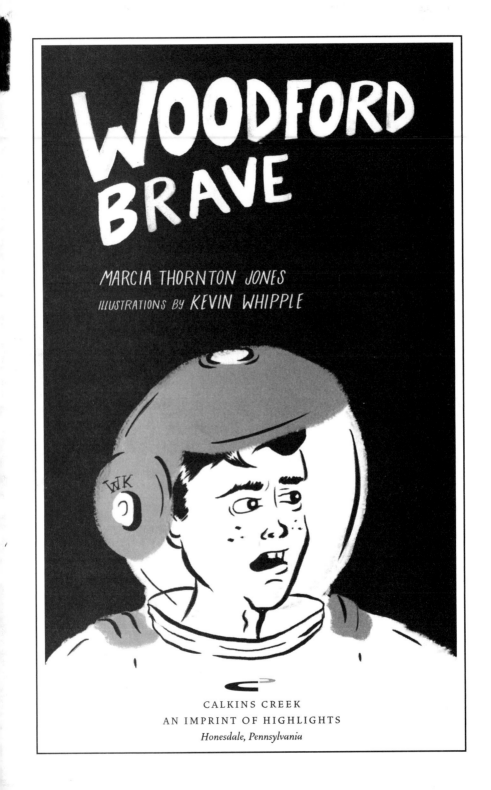

WOODFORD BRAVE

MARCIA THORNTON JONES

ILLUSTRATIONS BY KEVIN WHIPPLE

CALKINS CREEK
AN IMPRINT OF HIGHLIGHTS
Honesdale, Pennsylvania

Calkins Creek
An Imprint of Highlights
815 Church Street
Honesdale, Pennsylvania 18431

Printed in the United States of America
ISBN: 978-1-62979-305-4 (print)
ISBN: 978-1-62979-437-2 (e-book)
Library of Congress Control Number: 2015931599

First edition
The text of this book is set in Legacy Sans ITC.
Design by Barbara Grzeslo
Production by Sue Cole
10 9 8 7 6 5 4 3 2 1

To my mother, Thelma Thornton,
for sharing her stories;
and to my father, Robert Thornton,
a veteran of two wars.
—MTJ

THE SPY OF SATAN'S SIDEWALK

Anarrow strip of bushes was the only thing that separated Ziegler's yard from my hiding place in the old Mallory house. Mom had warned me that the floors of the haunted house were bound to collapse if I ever stepped foot inside, but rotten floors were the least of my worries. Not when there was a spy living in our town. It was up to me, and me alone, to save Harmony and everyone in it from the Nazi living at the bottom of Satan's Sidewalk. I knew it. Aidan knew it. And Sawyer knew it, even though he'd be the last one to admit it.

"I'm going to hog-tie Ziegler and turn him over to President Roosevelt," I told Aidan and Sawyer. "Then I'll be a hero just like—"

"We know, Cory. We know. Just because your last name is Woodford, you think you'll be like your dear old dad and grandpa. You don't have to keep grandstanding about it," Sawyer said.

He kept his voice low, but he didn't whisper, so the

dogs pacing the fence let loose with a tangle of growls and barks that curled the hair on my neck. Ziegler's wolf-hounds were not the typical wag-their-tails-and-lick-your-face type of dogs. They were the grab-your-throat-and-shake-you-till-you're-dead kind of beasts.

"Roosevelt said to keep our mouths shut and our eyes open because spies are everywhere," I reminded Sawyer. "Ziegler's one of them, I'm sure of it. I just need to catch him in the act."

Aidan's eyes were as wide as I'd ever seen them, but only because he was looking around the room for ghosts. Full summer dark was at least an hour away, but shadows already lurked in the corners of the old house. "Do you think this is where Cyn slept? Before she and her family were k-k-killed?" he asked.

My best friend's words always tripped over his tongue, but the thought of facing a house full of ghosts made it worse. I checked to make sure the latest edition of *The Cosmic Adventures of the Mighty Space Warrior* was rolled up safely in my back pocket. Not even the Warrior's StealthGrenades or Shield of Invisibility would help against ghosts. I didn't really believe in haunts anymore, but I knew Aidan still believed the story about how the Mallory family had become acid-oozing phantoms after their gruesome deaths.

"There is no such thing as ghosts," Sawyer said. "So get your foot out of the bucket and quit worrying."

The tips of Aidan's ears burned red at Sawyer's dig. Aidan

had been trying to impress Sawyer, the best baseball player in Harmony, ever since coming up with his lamebrain idea to make it to the Majors.

"But there *are* spies," I pointed out, turning my attention back to Ziegler's house. "If I had the Mighty Space Warrior's StealthGrenades, I'd lob them through Ziegler's window. Then I'd fire a subzero shock wave from my ray gun at his death hounds, freezing them in their evil tracks until they shattered into a gazillion pieces."

Sawyer hooted as if he didn't care that the wolfhounds below us were waiting to sink their teeth clear down to our bones. "You have about as much chance of being a superhero as you do of making the Majors, Cory."

It was no secret that Sawyer ate, breathed, and lived for baseball. It was also no secret that I was the worst player in town. I clenched my jaw the same way I'd seen Dad do. "If I *did* have the Warrior's superpowers, I'd turn Ziegler and his dogs into piles of ash. Then I'd hand you a broom and make *you* sweep them all up."

"Sweeping is for girls," Sawyer said. "Not baseball stars."

The air was thick and humid and sweat trickled down my back like molten lava from the Torch of Evil's home planet. From our hiding place in the upstairs window of the old haunted house, we could almost touch Ziegler's place. The maple tree was the only green thing in Ziegler's yard, since his two wolfhounds had worn away every blade of grass and nothing was left but sunbaked dirt. Especially in front of the short, rickety gate that looked like it was made of rotten Popsicle sticks. We called the alley Satan's Sidewalk, and the gate the Demons' Door, because of Ziegler and his dogs. There was no doubt in my mind that his hounds could soar over that gate in one giant leap to tear out my jugular.

I leaned out the broken window for a beeline view straight into Ziegler's dining room. A single lamp cast his face in deep shadows, turning his eye sockets into nothing but black holes. Sitting on the table before him was the beat-up leather case he always carried.

"The lid's blocking my view," I whispered. "I can't tell what's inside." Obviously, x-ray vision wasn't my superpower.

"I bet it's full of c-c-coded messages," Aidan said, squeezing beside me to get a peek.

"About what?" Sawyer asked. "We live in the podunk town of Harmony. There's nothing here a Nazi spy would want."

Sawyer hated Harmony. He said it was because our town wasn't big enough for a baseball team of our own, but I thought it was because Harmony was so small everyone knew his dad would rather belly-up to the bar at the corner tavern than enlist in the fight against Hitler.

"There's the VFW," I pointed out. The Veterans of Foreign Wars provided services for soldiers, and they had dinners and dances. Dad had taken Mom there the one time he was home on leave. "You've seen the posters. 'Loose lips sink ships!' That could happen if a soldier had one beer too many. Even here in Harmony."

"I hate the Nazis like everyone else, Cory, but this spy hunt is a waste of time." Sawyer spat like he always did when we talked about the Germans, as if the word left a bad taste in his mouth. But it was really because the gum he chewed created more spit than he could swallow. Sawyer thought the huge wad in his cheek made him look like Spuds Chandler or Joe DiMaggio. He'd been chewing the same wad for two weeks, saving it on the bedpost every night. Aidan tried the same thing, but his mom yelled at him about it ruining the paint. Now he wasn't allowed to have gum for the rest of the summer.

I pushed my Yankees cap firmly onto my head so it wouldn't fall out the window when I leaned out farther to get a better bead on Ziegler's case. That's when Sawyer shoved me.

I jumped. Not from being scared, but because a sliver of glass dug into the palm of my hand.

Sawyer nearly choked on his gum, he laughed so hard. "Admit it, Cory. I just scared the snot out of you!"

"Nuh-uh. I'm brave. I'm . . ."

"Yeah, yeah, yeah," Aidan said. "We all know. You're W-W-Woodford Brave."

I glared at my best friend while Sawyer slapped Aidan on the back.

"Watch out!" I yelped when Aidan almost toppled out the window. Of course, I forgot to keep my voice down and Ziegler's dogs let loose with a volley of barks loud enough to wake the dead. Which wasn't a good thing, considering we were hiding in a haunted house.

We hit the floor when Ziegler glanced out his window. Ten seconds later we heard his back door open, followed by his voice, with its thick German accent. "Odin. Pandora. *Komm!*"

I snatched the Yankees cap off my head so it wouldn't give me away when I peeked over the sill. My head felt vulnerable in the air, like the Space Warrior without his Shield of Invisibility. Or my father without his Army helmet.

At the sound of Ziegler's command, his two giant dogs loped away from their watch at the fence

"Good! Good!" Ziegler said as he held open the door for them. "*Braver Hund!*"

A few seconds later, I saw them trot past the dining room window. I held my breath when Ziegler made his way around the table, looking outside for a heartbeat before dropping the blackout curtains.

I slapped my cap on the windowsill. "If it wasn't for you, we would've seen all those top-secret spy papers and I'd have my proof," I told Sawyer.

"You're the one who forgot to whisper," he said. "Admit it, Cory. Your plan to prove Ziegler is a Nazi spy is nothing but a swing and a miss."

"We c-c-couldn't see anything from up here, anyway," Aidan interrupted, trying to keep Sawyer and me from getting into it. Again.

"Shh," I hissed.

"It doesn't matter, C-C-Cory," Aidan argued. "It's too late. Z-Z-Ziegler's gone."

"*Shh*," I said, holding up my hand to silence them. "Someone . . . or some*thing* . . . is in here with us."

That's when they heard it, too. Thumping. Right over our heads.

"It's probably a b-b-branch scraping the siding," Aidan said, his voice rising in a question.

I glanced out the window. The air was a heavy wet blanket. Nothing moved. Not even a leaf.

Thump.

Thump.

Scrrrrritch.

"There's only one thing that c-c-could be," Aidan whispered.

Sawyer looked at the ceiling, then at Aidan. They both turned to me. I was the only one brave enough to say the word that was on all our minds. "Ghosts!"

Sawyer shoved Aidan aside and jumped for the stairs. Aidan and I scrambled after him, jamming ourselves in the narrow door opening until Aidan finally pushed through. "Go, go, GO!" I urged, shoving on my best friend's back.

A board gave way, trapping my foot, and all those

warnings from Mom flooded my brain as I pulled and tugged and jerked until my foot broke loose, ripping a piece of skin off my ankle. Sawyer jumped down the last five steps, landed on the first floor, slipped, and ricocheted off a wall. Aidan rammed into his back. Their feet tangled and Aidan fell to one knee. I grabbed his arm before he went down.

Sawyer pushed off Aidan, stumbling toward the back door in a half-crouch, fighting for balance with every step. We jumped out the door a half-second after him and hit the ground running, racing for the safety of the alley.

Wham! Aidan pulled up short and Sawyer collided into him, knocking both of them to the ground.

Wham! I tripped over Sawyer and fell headfirst into the very thing that had stopped Aidan cold.

Aidan rolled to one side and Sawyer tried to butt-scoot back. Not me. A hero always holds his ground. Besides, Sawyer had me blocked, so there was nothing I could do but look straight into the eyes of the man I'd just knocked down.

Ziegler.

2

BLOOD OF THE BRAVE

Ziegler sat on Satan's Sidewalk clutching the black case to his chest as if he were protecting a baby. "You! What are you doing in that abandoned house?" His heavy accent made it sound more like "Vhat are you doink?"

The Space Warrior would've ripped the case from his hands, pried it open, and flung his Nazi secrets into the hot August air. But I wasn't the Warrior, and I knew Mom would swat my behind if I was rude. Even if Ziegler was German.

"We're s-s-sorry," I muttered, sounding more like Aidan than myself. Apologizing to a spy settled a vile taste on my tongue, and I fought the urge to spit like Sawyer. "We didn't mean to knock you down."

Ziegler used his left hand to push off the ground, but his right hand still clutched the black case. He stood tall and dark against the backdrop of the alley. He looked down his nose at us, straightening his wire-rimmed glasses to see me better. "Itz dangerous place to play in there. You should know better. Ztay away from that house."

I didn't move a muscle, waiting until he'd made it to the end of the alley and turned left up Catalpa before daring to talk. "Did you hear that? Ziegler *threatened* us."

"M-M-Maybe he's just trying to keep us safe from whoever . . . or . . . whatever was sneaking up on us," Aidan said.

We glanced back at the haunted house. The sun had dipped low in the sky, coating the Mallory yard in shadows, but there was just enough light to see a scrawny yellow cat hop out the back door.

Sawyer burst out laughing. "Mr. Cory-The-Almighty-Brave-Woodford was scared of an itty-bitty kitty-cat!"

"Was not."

"Were, too," Sawyer said. "You ran so fast sparks flew from your shoes."

"You're the one who pushed us out of the way in order to high-tail it out first. I was following you, that's all," I said.

"I'm not afraid of a stupid cat," Sawyer said. "I'll catch him and wring his mangy little neck to prove it."

When he stepped back into the Mallory yard, the cat froze with one foot in the air. I reached out and grabbed Sawyer's arm. "He's not the enemy. Ziegler is."

For a minute, the setting sun reflecting off Sawyer's eyes made him look as evil as a Mallory ghost, but then he shrugged off my hand and snatched my comic book off the ground where it had fallen. "You know you're nothing like this stupid superhero. Being scared of a cat proves that."

I grabbed my comic book, carefully rolling it up again so the cover wouldn't crease, before I said what the Space Warrior says in the face of danger. "I don't know the meaning of fear."

"That's what you always s-s-say," Aidan said.

I was sick of not being taken seriously, of always having to prove myself. I was tired of the way my best friend laughed when Sawyer made fun of me, and how they both acted like the fact that my grandfather and father were war heroes had absolutely nothing to do with me. My veins carried the blood of the brave and they knew it, but before I got the chance to utter another word, a Ford flatbed piled with a kitchen table, chairs, a sofa, and boxes rumbled up Catalpa.

"It's the n-n-new neighbors," Aidan hollered.

"Let's go!" Sawyer snatched his glove and bat off the ground where he'd dumped them, and they both took off together, leaving me standing alone in the shadows of the Nazi's lair.

Speed definitely wasn't my superpower, and my shirt was sweat-plastered to my back by the time I climbed the hill to the top of Satan's Sidewalk. Jackson sat on the worn step leading to the back door of Aidan's house. The music of Glenn Miller and his orchestra floated through the screen door, the trumpet's brass marching over the strings.

Most people listened to the radio for war news, keeping maps on their walls and following the Allied troops using different colored pins. They made a mess of holes in the walls, but no one cared. There were other war reports, too. Just last night there was one about the horrible conditions in the concentration camps that the Nazis were using for the Jews and anybody else they didn't like. People were crowded into the camps without enough food and water even though they hadn't done anything wrong. It was the kind of story that made my skin crawl and made me glad Dad was over there stopping the Nazis.

Jackson was the only person I knew who tuned in to music instead of news. His foot tapped and his head bopped to the beat.

Aidan always seemed to grow three inches around his brother, but Jackson nodded at me as if he didn't notice Aidan. "Heard from your dad, Cory?" Jackson asked.

Sometimes we wouldn't hear from Dad for weeks. Mom would be a nervous wreck. Then we'd get a bundle of letters all at once with sentences and entire paragraphs blacked out by censors in case the letters were intercepted by enemy spies. "Got three letters yesterday."

"Any idea where he is?"

"Way north of Italy. But that was before the battle of Palermo."

We had all sat spellbound the month before, listening to Edward Murrow reporting from Europe on the CBS

World News Roundup radio show as Patton led Allied troops into Italy. But Hitler was the real enemy. Dad was probably dodging bombs, jumping over trenches, and ignoring bullets as he led a battalion north toward Hitler's lair in Germany. That's what a hero would do.

"He kill anybody yet?" I noticed Jackson's Adam's apple seemed to hiccup when he asked it.

I shrugged. People died in wars, and if people died then someone had to be doing the killing, but that was the kind of information the censors blacked out.

"J-J-Jackson can't wait to get over there," Aidan butted in.

Aidan's brother turned eighteen in a month, which meant he would do what every other red-blooded-true-blue American would do: enlist. Just like my dad had done. Since Aidan's dad couldn't enlist on account of his busted-up knee, all Aidan talked about was how Jackson was going to win the war single-handedly once he got over there. Hearing about it was getting as tiresome as Hitler's blitzkrieg bombings of London.

The music from Glenn Miller's Orchestra floating out the open windows gave way to Bing Crosby. "The Crooner," they called him. Jackson scratched his head right where the hair was starting to curl over his collar, then got distracted by the truck that had circled the block and was heading down the alley, its brakes grinding to a stop in front of what used to be the Taylors' garage.

When the Taylors lived next door to Aidan, they'd hung a blue star in the window for their son just like Mom did after Dad went to Europe. Only Mom made a star out of old wrapping paper left over from Christmas and taped it to the window, and Mrs. Taylor ordered a special-made banner with the blue star sewn dead-center on it. After their son was killed, she stitched a gold one over the blue. Blue for the living. Gold for the dead. It didn't hang in their window for long because Mr. Taylor lost his job at the grain elevator and they moved to Burlington. The house had been empty ever since. Until now.

"Wonder who the new folks are," Jackson said. He said it mostly to himself, but Aidan acted like his brother had just handed him a secret mission.

"We'll find out!" Aidan ran straight to the maple tree in the corner of his yard, climbing up to the platform Jackson had helped us nail between two limbs the summer before last. It wasn't much of a tree house, but until this summer, when Aidan had gotten all buddy-buddy with Sawyer, it had been our secret hangout.

Sawyer beat me to the tree and scrambled up after Aidan. There wasn't enough room in the tree house for three, so I perched on a lower limb, rested my back against the trunk, and tried to see all the way to Ziegler's house at the bottom of the hill.

The bushes surrounding Ziegler's yard were so high a tank wouldn't be able to see over them. Sawyer was right about one thing—I didn't have proof that Ziegler was a spy. But the fact that he was from Germany was enough to make me suspect he might be part of Hitler's inner circle. Since I had promised Dad I'd keep Mom safe until he got home from stopping the Nazi aggression in Europe, it was obviously up to me to expose Ziegler for what he really was and save the entire town.

My other next-door neighbor, Mrs. Springgate, sat on her porch, her white hair flopping with every flutter of the cardboard fan in her hand. She was probably getting snookered on beer again. It was hard to tell since beer cans were rationed and she had switched to drinking from glass jars, but it was a known fact that since her husband died she preferred sipping beer to drinking milk.

Mom was working in her Victory Garden, staking up the tomatoes. Growing vegetables was never going to help us win the war, no matter what Mrs. Roosevelt said. There was no way a bombardment of tomatoes and squash could stop Hitler or his evil spies.

"I hope there's a k-k-kid our age," Aidan was saying.

"One who plays ball," Sawyer added. "We need some-one who can really step up to the plate."

There it was again. Baseball. Sawyer's favorite thing in the whole wide world. I checked to see if he was looking at me. He was.

The new neighbors spilled out of the truck and were already unloading boxes from the back. If I squinted

I could make out the "A" sticker on the windshield showing their gas-rationing allocation. "There's a bald guy and an old lady," I said. "And a girl."

Sawyer groaned. "Girls don't count. All they think about are dresses and lace and dolls."

"This one isn't wearing frilly stuff," I pointed out. "She looks to be wearing overalls and Keds."

Sawyer leaned back against the trunk of the tree, already bored. "Doesn't matter. Girls can't pitch and they can't hit. By morning she'll be prissing down the street wearing ribbons and carrying a doll-baby. Mark my words."

"G-G-Girls are useless when it comes to b-b-baseball," Aidan said with a shake of his head.

As if to punctuate his words something *whomped* the bark right above Aidan's head. He jerked, slipping over the edge of our tree house. His arms flailed, searching for a handhold. Anything to stop his fall. He grabbed a branch, stripping leaves as his grip slipped.

"Help!" he yelped, clutching for Sawyer. Only Sawyer didn't reach out fast enough to stop my best friend from falling headfirst out of the tree.

3

A BASEBALL PEACH

Aidan slammed against the branch next to me, caught on another branch, then slid until his pants snagged a limb. I did what any hero would do—reached out and grabbed his shirt to keep him from getting his pants torn clean off. I was saving his life, but did Aidan notice? No sir-ee. He slapped my hand away and slid the rest of the way down.

The new girl stood on Satan's Sidewalk watching everything, a slingshot in her hand. The sun filtering through leaves reflected off her blue eyes. Not that the color of her eyes made any difference.

"What are you doing?" she asked. "Spying on us?"

"Shh," I hissed, glancing down Satan's Sidewalk even though Ziegler was too far away to hear. "'Loose lips sink ships!'"

"Don't pay attention to Cory," Sawyer said, hopping down on the other side of Aidan and landing with both feet in a dust cloud. "He's a big knuckleball."

If only I had jets on my boots like the Space Warrior's,

I could've flown from the tree like a true hero. Instead, I scrambled down, ignoring the long scrape the bark left on my knee next to the scratch I'd earned escaping the Mallory house. Once on the ground I reached back to make sure *The Cosmic Adventures of the Mighty Space Warrior* hadn't gotten ripped on tree bark.

"What's your name?" Sawyer asked with about as much politeness as a pig in a trough.

"Anya . . . I mean, Anne," she said. "Anne Burke."

Sawyer squinted as if he'd just caught Anne throwing a spitball. "Don't you know your own name?"

"Of course I do. It's Anne. Just like I said."

"You said An-*ya.*"

Anne rolled her eyes. "My tongue slipped. That's all. We're from Joliet. That's in Illinois near Chicago, right here in the good ol' U.S. of A. Joliet is a big city compared to Harmony."

"That probably means your dad's a Cubs fan."

Leave it to Sawyer to start talking about baseball.

Anne had her hands on her hips, dangling the slingshot from its rubber sling. "Of course not, because the Cardinals are the best team in the whole wide world."

Sawyer sputtered. "Nuh-uh. The Yankees are."

She set her chin so it jutted out by at least an inch and eyeballed my Yankees cap. Anne didn't wear her hair in any bows, so when a loose strand curled around her cheek and stuck to her lip, she blew it away. "The Cardinals won the World Series, so that makes them the best."

Mom would've swatted the seat of my pants if I didn't show better manners to our new neighbors than Sawyer, so I stopped him before he could pick a full-fledged fight. "That's Sawyer and this is Aidan. He's your next-door neighbor. Sawyer lives two blocks to the north. I'm Cory. I live across Satan's Sidewalk."

"Satan's Sidewalk?" Anne repeated, her blue eyes suddenly losing their squint and turning big and round. "What's that?"

"What Cory calls the alley you're standing on," Sawyer said, butting in before I had a chance to explain. His one-track brain was in full gear and he couldn't be bothered with manners. "Got any brothers? Someone our age? Someone who can pitch and hit?"

Anne shook her head. "It's just me, Dad, and Grandma. My mom's dead, but don't worry. I'm not sad anymore. Not much, anyway. She's been dead for almost two years."

Sawyer pointed to the slingshot. "Well, if you don't have any brothers, who does that belong to?"

"Me," she said, smiling so big the freckles on her nose got all squished together. "Dad taught me how to make one. I'm good at building stuff. Someday I'm going to build houses and stores and maybe even skyscrapers like in New York City."

"Nuh-uh. You're a girl. Girls grow up to have babies and cook turkeys," Sawyer told her, as if it was the eleventh commandment.

"You're the turkey," Anne said, and I grinned at the way

she didn't back down from Sawyer. "Being a girl doesn't matter. Just ask Rosie the Riveter. It's what a person does, not what they are, that's important. And I can do anything I want. I can already saw wood, patch bike tires, and pitch a mean fastball, too. I want to be a Peach. A Rockford Peach."

"That's not a *real* team," Sawyer argued.

"Is, too."

"Not."

"Yes, it is," Anne said with a tiny stomp of her Keds. "Dad took me to a game before we left Joliet. Olive Little pitches a fastball that could spin your head like a corkscrew, and I'm going to be just like her. I'm already a better baseball player than most boys. I bet I'm every bit as good as you."

"Imp-p-possible," Aidan said. "Sawyer is p-p-practicing for the Majors. Tell her she's f-f-full of beans, Cory."

They were all looking at me, waiting for an answer. Cory and Aidan on one side, Anne on the other. Sawyer's face had turned so red he could've been the Torch of Evil's long-lost cousin, and Anne's cheeks were dotted with pink.

I said what I had to say. "He's the best player in all of Harmony. Ask anyone."

Sawyer slapped me on the shoulder so hard I had to take three steps to keep from falling headfirst onto Satan's Sidewalk. Something about the way the new girl looked at me made me feel worse than if I had just admitted to being in cahoots with the double-crossing spy living at the bottom of Satan's Sidewalk.

THE ADVENTURES OF THE WARRIOR KID

4

My room was stifling that night. Blackout curtains hid the lights so our house couldn't be spotted by enemy planes, but they also kept out any trace of a breeze. I wiped a bead of sweat from my head and started to write.

Dear Dad,

A new girl moved into the Taylor house, and guess what! She's a Cardinals fan! It was enough for Sawyer to hate Anne right on the spot. Who knew girls even cared about baseball? She doesn't bat an eyelash over the way Aidan's words get tangled on his tongue, and she's got freckles on her cheek that look like a constellation. Not that I care about stuff like a girl's freckles or anything. It's just something I noticed, that's all.

Sawyer's still ticked over the Yankees

losing to the Cardinals. I wear the Yankees cap you bought me every day, and I see him eyeballing it. I know he wishes he had one just like it, but that doesn't make up for him being such a fat-head. He nearly choked on his gum when Anne told us she wants to play for the Peaches. He thinks the only reason they started the All-American Girls Professional Baseball League is because the Majors' season might be cancelled now that most players are enlisting. Baseball. It's all Aidan talks about now that he's teamed up with Sawyer. That, and how his brother is going to win the war single-handedly. Sawyer calls baseball players heroes, but he's wrong.

I know

you're

the real hero!

I couldn't tell Dad about the Nazi spy living down the alley and how I planned to catch him red-handed, because of the censors who read all the letters.

I glanced at the Space Warrior grinning up at me with his cobalt-blue eyes from the cover of my comic book. His red x-ray goggles blasted yellow death rays, and lightning bolts zigzagged from his blue-gloved fists of doom. The Warrior, with his sidekick the Allied Panther, faced yet another attack from the Torch of Evil, a hideous being made of nothing but red-purple flames.

It truly was a beautiful picture.

There was plenty of space left on the paper beneath my letter, so I started to draw my own comic strip. My superhero was smaller than the Space Warrior, and the initials on the sides of his Helmet of Power were "WK." Short for "Warrior's Kid."

WAVES EMANATED FROM THE KID'S HELMET
OF POWER—A HELMET GIVEN TO HIM BY
HIS FATHER THE WARRIOR.
AS LONG AS HE WORE THE HELMET, THE KID WAS INDESTRUCTIBLE. THE KID DID
NOT FLINCH. HE DID NOT WAVER. HIS MUSCLES BULGED AND HIS CAPE BILLOWED.

HIS HYPERSPEED BOOTS LEFT CRATERS ON THE SURFACE OF THE RUINED PLANET.

THE SPY EXPLODED A BOULDER INTO DUST. THE KID MARCHED FEARLESSLY ON.

A MOUNTAIN BEHIND THE KID'S BACK WENT UP IN A PUFF OF ACID SMOKE.

THE KID DID NOT FALTER. TWO SCRAWNY BOYS SHIELDED THEIR FACES WITH BASEBALL MITTS... ONE BOY JUST HAPPENED TO HAVE CHEEKS BULGING WITH GUM, AND THE OTHER HAD LOPSIDED EARS. "SAVE US, KID! SAVE US!" THEY CRIED.

THE KID, HIS FINGERS CURLED INTO A FIST THE SIZE OF A TANK, DREW THE WARRIOR'S STRENGTH FROM HIS HELMET OF POWER. HE SMASHED THE EVIL SPY UNDER THE CHIN,

SENDING HIM SOMERSAULTING INTO THE BLACKNESS OF SPACE UNTIL HE WAS NOTHING BUT A SPECK.

I looked over my comic strip, wondering if Dad would notice that I had drawn my own face tucked inside the superhero's Helmet of Power.

LAST WORDS

Thwok. A pebble smacked against the garage. If I hadn't been bending over Mom's tomato plants, it would've binged me in the head.

Thwok.

Another one hit the tomato I was ready to pluck. The skin cracked, bleeding tomato juice.

THWOK!

Something smacked into the seat of my pants with enough force that I was sure it left a bruise the size of Italy's boot.

I faced the alley. "Cut it out!"

Sawyer and Aidan were in the tree house. It bothered me that they hadn't waited to make slingshots. Now I'd have to make my own, though there really wasn't enough room in my pocket for both a slingshot and my comic book.

I plucked tomatoes from the vines, imagining loading a slingshot of epic proportions with supercharged explosives powerful enough to knock the Mallory ghosts clean off the planet. The slingshot would work on the demon dogs, too. And once the dogs were out of the way, I'd use it to whop Ziegler until his eyeballs rolled up into his head. Then I'd hog-tie him with a red-white-and-blue bow and slingshot him all the way to the White House. Sawyer wouldn't dare say my veins were dry of Woodford blood then.

But I couldn't save the world, because Mom was inside, listening to the radio and waiting for tomatoes. Every so often the sounds of Les Brown, Doris Day, and Bing Crosby were interrupted by updates of battles and troop movements on the European and Pacific fronts. Then Mom would drop everything and run into the living room to turn up the volume. Earlier there had been a report that Nazi concentration camps were worse than anyone could imagine. Much worse. People were being rounded up, starved, and killed. I didn't get to hear the whole story, though, since Mom turned down the volume. She hated the stories about the camps. Everyone did. What the Nazis were doing was wrong. They had to be stopped. And my dad was right in the thick of the war to do just that.

Walking into the kitchen was like being bear-hugged by the Torch of Evil. Even though the blackout curtains were pushed aside and the windows were open as wide as they would go, there wasn't a hint of a breeze. "How can you stand it in here?" I asked.

Mom pushed aside a strand of limp hair. "If canning

tomatoes helps the war effort just a little, then we'll do it, Cory. Anything to help get your father home."

"He'll come home a hero, too," I said. "Just like Grandpa. Everybody in town says so."

Mom looked at me, and for a minute I thought she was going to snap off my head like a tomato from the vine. "But Dad'll come back alive," I added fast.

Mom let out a breath and squeezed my shoulder in a sideways hug. "Of course he will," she said. "He promised." She sorted through the tomatoes, picking out five of the best ones. "Take these over to the new neighbors. Let them know I'm canning jars for them, too."

Stepping out into the August sun should've felt hot, but after being in the kitchen it was a relief.

The way Sawyer leaned against Aidan's garage made it look like he was trying to push it over. Sawyer's bat was propped against the fence and his mitt sat on top of it. Sawyer would've carried his bat and glove to church if his mom let him.

"Let's p-p-play ball," Aidan shouted loud enough to scare a mockingbird from the maple tree.

I held up the tomatoes. "I have to give these to the new neighbors." Then, as an afterthought, I added, "Maybe Anne will want to tag along."

"Your girlfriend would rather play with her doll-babies, but you could stay here and play house with her," Sawyer said with a grin. He had a rock the size of my thumb pulled back in his slingshot, ready to let it fly at the mockingbird that had landed on top of Aidan's garage.

"She's not my girlfriend," I said, hating the way my face felt as if I'd been spat on by the Torch of Evil himself. "I'm just being neighborly, that's all."

"Sounds like love to me," Sawyer said, laughing so hard the rock he sent flying went wide right. The bird took flight anyway, proving it was smarter than Sawyer and all the kissy-kissy noises he started making.

Aidan rode the gate as it swung open to the Burkes' yard. He laughed as if Sawyer was funnier than Daffy Duck while I made my way across the backyard to Anne's door. She opened it before I even knocked. Just like before, she wore overalls and Keds. There wasn't a bow or doll in sight. Nothing pink, either. Except for her cheeks. She squinted at Sawyer holding his bat over his shoulder the way a soldier carries a gun. "I'll get my mitt."

I stuck out the bag of tomatoes. "These are for your family. I'm supposed to tell your grandmother that my mom will can tomatoes for you, too."

Anne grabbed the bag. "I'll tell her. Wait here. I'll tell her everything." Then she closed the door and left me standing on the back step.

Sawyer sauntered across the yard and hopped up the steps next to me. Aidan followed him like a little puppy dog, only there wasn't enough room on the step, so he had to stand in the grass. "Of all the nerve," Sawyer said. "A dumb Dora of a girl, thinking she can play as good as me. That's the stupidest idea ever."

"You g-g-got that right," Aidan said.

"What's so stupid about it?" I asked. "She's got two arms to swing a bat just the same as you and me."

"You just say that because you think she's cute," Sawyer said.

"Do not," I sputtered.

"Do so," Sawyer shot right back. "But girly arms are weak. Not strong like ours." He punched my arm to prove his point, leaving a bruise clear down to the bone. I hated the fact that I flinched, and hated it even more that Sawyer noticed. But the worst thing was that Aidan laughed right along with Sawyer.

Sawyer was rubbing my nerves blood-raw, but Anne opened the door then, carrying a mitt that looked like it had been through the Great War. Aidan fell into step beside Sawyer as he led us around to the front of the houses so we didn't have to worry about Ziegler's dogs leaping the Demons' Door to tear out our throats. Aidan and Sawyer walked shoulder-to-shoulder which meant there wasn't enough room on the sidewalk for Anne and me. Anne acted like following them didn't bother her, but I figured it did, because of the way she stomped on their shadows.

The town square where we played was nothing more than a patch of grass surrounded by the Corner Tap, Franklin's Drug Emporium, the post office, Nelson's Funeral Hall, Swanson's Grocer, and Nichols's Hardware. Posters for war bonds plastered the boarded-up windows on the rest of the stores, which had all closed during the years leading up to the war. Crisscrossing sidewalks connected the four corners of the town square and met in the middle, where they circled around the statue of a soldier. Tall and stiff, he stood at attention as if standing guard over all of Harmony.

The first thing Anne did was squint up at the statue. "Who's that?"

Sawyer followed her gaze. "Aw, cripes. Don't get Cory started."

"My grandfather," I said, ignoring him, even though I knew full well ignoring Sawyer never worked.

The square was empty except for old Mrs. Baird, who acted like it was her sworn duty to spend afternoons in the park digging up dandelions with a rusted old soup spoon. Just seeing her made me remember walking with Dad across the square when I was a little kid. We had paused to look up at my grandfather's face, lost in a halo of sunshine. The way his head touched the sky made me think the statue was tall enough to reach up and grab a passing cloud.

That day, Mrs. Baird's spoon had been crusty with dirt. A mutilated worm dangled from the handle, writhing in front of my nose. Dad wanted me to look at her, to say something polite. He squeezed my hand so hard my bones crunched, but I couldn't move. My eyes were locked on the dying struggle of that worm. It hung, suspended for a split second, curling up as if trying to reach out for me. Then it lost its grip on the tarnished silver. I pulled away from

Dad's hand, hopping back so the worm wouldn't splat on my shoe.

"Don't you worry," Mrs. Baird had said. "That ugly ol' thing can't hurt you."

There was the sound of a smile in her voice, but I couldn't know for sure since my eyes were still on the worm, watching as it twitched one last time.

"Don't be silly, Cory," Dad had said, and I could tell by the sound of his voice he was disappointed in me. "It's just a worm."

That was the day I swore I'd never embarrass him again. I'd never show the least hint of fear. Ever. I would be like him. And Grandpa. Woodford Brave.

Anne shaded her eyes with one hand, blocking out the sun to get a better look at my grandfather's stony face. "He looks a little like you. Tell me about him."

"He was a hero. Not like the Mighty Space Warrior or Captain America, since he didn't have superpowers. But he died saving a bunch of men during the Great War."

"I didn't mean the part about how he died," she said. "How did he live? Did he collect stamps? Did he like to play checkers? Did he snort when he laughed?"

I opened my mouth, then shut it fast when it occurred to me that I didn't have the foggiest idea. I had grown up hearing how Grandpa went to war and saved a lot of men. How he suffered from mustard gas and died a painful death. That made him a hero, and that was that. Everybody said so. "I'm sure he was brave his whole life," I finally said. "Just like my dad."

"Too bad everyone remembers him for the way he died," Anne said. "I mean, what if your grandpa was just a normal kind of person but he died doing one great thing? It seems how a person lived should be more important than one single deed."

"All that is ancient history," Sawyer interrupted, proving yet again that ignoring him didn't work one iota. "Are you ready to play, or are you just stalling because you know I'm going to beat the freckles off your nose?"

Anne stepped up to the dirt patch that was our pitcher's mound. "Cory and I will take on you and Aidan. You're up first."

"You really think you can pitch it in the wheelhouse?" Sawyer asked Anne.

"I don't *think* it. I *know* it."

"This ought to be good for a laugh," Sawyer said, jogging to take his place at the worn-out dirt patch that was our home plate. I took the catcher's position and Aidan headed across the park, figuring Sawyer would slam that ball to kingdom come, but he was wrong. It took only four of Anne's pitches to prove that Sawyer wasn't the only one who had a fastball guaranteed to take the skin off your nose.

"Strrrrr-iiiiike three," she yelled. "You're OUT!"

It was the first time anyone had ever said those two words to Sawyer. His face was red, and sweat rolled down the sides of his face. He was hot, all right, but not from swinging at the ball. He let the bat hit the ground with a hollow bounce before switching places with Aidan.

Aidan held the bat just like Sawyer had coached. When he popped a ball toward the dirt patch we called third base, Anne sprinted over and caught it before it had a chance to bounce in the grass.

Aidan looked at Sawyer with eyes that would've made a hound dog seem downright cheerful. Sawyer didn't notice. He was too busy glaring at Anne in a way that would freeze the Torch of Evil in his tracks.

Anne took her turn at home plate, the bat hovering over her right shoulder. I expected Sawyer to throw a beanball, but Sawyer eyed the spot in front of her shoulders, wound up, then let a fastball rip. Anne didn't move a muscle until the ball crossed the plate. Then she swung. Hard. The bat hit the ball with a crack that should've shattered windows. It sailed back over Sawyer's head, over Grandpa's statue, and clear to the other side of the square.

"Wa-hooooooooo!" I shouted without thinking.

Sawyer spat on the ground and glared at me. "Nothing but luck," he said.

"Admit it," Anne said, holding safe at third, "I'm better than you."

I barely had time to snatch the bat out of the air when Sawyer tossed it to me.

All ball players had good luck habits. I was no different. I patted the latest edition of the Space Warrior comic book riding in my hip pocket, then tugged on the bill of my lucky ball cap. I imagined becoming the Kid from my comic strip. My arms, rippled with muscles, effortlessly hoisted the bat high, ready to hit a torpedo of doom over the Atlantic Ocean to where the Warrior was surrounded by the Torch and his evil henchmen.

Sawyer smacked the ball in his mitt, obviously itching to prove he was better than a dumb Dora. He wound up and sent a fastball straight for my heart, making sure to put extra smoke in the pitch. Instinct, not fear, made me dodge. I stumbled, tripped on my own left foot, and fell down on my keister.

Sawyer shouted loud enough to wake the Mallory ghosts. "Strrrr-iiiiiiiike one!"

The first thing I did when I got up was to make sure I hadn't torn the cover of my comic book. The next thing was to glare at Sawyer. "You did that on purpose."

"I'd never beanball you, Cory," Sawyer said. "But I bet that Space Warrior of yours wouldn't play with his foot in the bucket the way you do. This time, stare the ball down and wait to swing until it's close enough to kiss. Think of it as Anne."

Aidan hooted at that and Anne rolled her eyes. I made sure my cap was down over my ears and then waited, waited, waited. Just before Sawyer's pitch sailed past me, I swung. My arms jolted with the crack of the bat when it smashed the ball, but my hit went high and wild, bouncing off my grandfather's nose with a sharp *thunk* before ricocheting across the park.

"D-D-Duck!" Aidan yelled, barely getting the word out in time.

Mrs. Baird fell flat on the grass as the ball breezed over her flowery straw hat. Sawyer doubled over, almost swallowing his gum, he laughed so hard.

Aidan reached Mrs. Baird first and was quick to help her up. "I'm sorry," I told her, jogging up beside Aidan. "I wasn't aiming for you. Really, I wasn't."

Mrs. Baird eyed me over the tops of her sweat-dotted glasses. Gray hair had sprung loose and a clump of grass was stuck in her straw hat. I couldn't help but check out her rusty spoon for worms. There weren't any.

"You should have more respect for your grandfather's memory," she huffed, pulling down her dress. "He deserves better than to be smacked in the nose with a baseball."

The base of the statue was cool and solid under my hand when I patted it. "Grandpa died a hero and my dad is just like him. A hero, I mean. Not dead. A hero for fighting the Nazi aggression."

Then I added the obvious. "I'm like him, too. My dad, I mean. Not Hitler. I'm brave. Woodford Brave."

Mrs. Baird looked like she was going to lecture me all the way to kingdom come, but instead, she thumped me on top of my cap with her spoon before grabbing her paper sack full of dandelion greens from Anne and marching to the far side of the square.

Sawyer shifted the wad of gum from one cheek to

the other, watching her go. "You know, being a hero isn't something that runs in families, Cory. It's not like being fat or skinny or having freckles."

"What's that supposed to mean?" I asked.

"Just what I said. You talk like some big crackerjack, but the truth is actions speak louder than words ever will. And you *act* like a chicken."

Anne tossed the ball into her mitt, her eyes moving back and forth between us. I wasn't about to let Sawyer make me look like some kind of fool in front of the new girl. Not that it mattered what a girl thought. No sir-ee. But with Dad fighting the Nazis, it was up to me to uphold the Woodford name. "Everyone in Harmony knows I'm brave just like my dad and my grandfather," I said. "Tell him, Aidan."

Aidan knew me better than anyone, considering we'd been best friends forever. That's why I couldn't believe it when he took a step. It was a tiny one, but it was big enough to move him closer to Sawyer than to me.

Sawyer didn't say anything. He didn't need to. He grinned around his wad of gum, then turned his back on my grandfather's statue and headed for home.

6

THE DEMONS' DOOR

nne kept talking a blue streak as if nothing out of the ordinary had happened. "Is your dad in the Pacific or on the European front? My dad supports the war, but he has flat feet or else he would've enlisted. Back in Illinois, I was a member of a club and collected a wagon full of old tin."

"So did we," I told her when she finally took a breath. "Aidan and I were members of Captain America's Sentinels of Liberty Club, even though I like the Space Warrior comic books better. We pulled Aidan's wagon halfway across Harmony collecting old newspapers."

Most kids in Harmony had collected tin, scrap material, and even our mothers' silk stockings. Metal to be melted down for ships and bullets. Material to be made into bandages and uniforms. Silk to make parachutes. Everything went toward winning the war.

"That was b-b-back when we were little kids," Aidan said over his shoulder, as if he were some kind of grownup all of a sudden. "We wanted to join the B-B-Boy Scouts of America but Mr. Dunne enlisted and there weren't any other dads around willing to be leaders so the Harmony troop f-f-fizzled."

Aidan didn't tell her that his own dad used his busted-up leg as an excuse not to volunteer. Or that Sawyer's dad had offered, but by the time he sobered up he had forgotten.

"I would've gotten a badge for collecting the most tin, but we had to leave Joliet, so I never did get it," Anne said.

"What do you mean you *had* to leave?" Sawyer asked.

Anne's mouth opened and shut, making her look like a catfish blowing bubbles. "I meant we *decided* to move. My dad used to own a store, but he got a better job working as a manager at Nichols's Hardware. Managing is much easier than owning. He's been in the hardware business longer than Hitler has been stirring up trouble in Germany. Dad wanted to join the Navy, and I think he'd look good in a sailor's uniform, but he has those flat feet and all."

When we reached the alley that paralleled Catalpa, Anne barreled onto it as if she didn't have a care in the world. I reached out and grabbed her arm without thinking. "Shh. You have to be quiet on Satan's Sidewalk."

Anne squinted into the shadows. "You never did tell me why you call the alley that."

"Because of the Demons' Door," I told her as if that explained it all.

"Demons' Door?" Anne repeated.

"The gate to Ziegler's yard," Sawyer answered before I

had a chance. "Cory thinks Ziegler is some kind of enemy spy."

"What makes you think he's a Nazi?" Anne asked.

"That's easy," I told her. "He's straight from Germany."

"You're a bunch of knuckleheads," she said. "Just because he's from Germany, it doesn't mean he's a Nazi."

"It's more than just his accent," I told her. "He carries a case and goes off on secret missions. We've seen him. And he has trained dogs guarding his house."

"Cory's afraid of puppy dogs," Sawyer added.

"Am not," I snapped. I wasn't about to let Sawyer paint me yellow in front of the new girl.

"Z-Z-Ziegler's dogs aren't puppies. They're the kind of dogs the d-d-devil himself would keep," Aidan added.

"I'm still not afraid of them," I muttered.

Sawyer met my gaze for a full ten seconds before a slow smile turned up his lips. "Then you won't be too scared to *show* your new girlfriend some of that Woodford Bravery, right, Cory?"

"She's not my girlfriend," I blurted. I didn't know what bothered me more. The fact that Sawyer said it, or the way Anne waved away his words as if they were nothing more than the stink of cigar smoke. I couldn't worry about it, because Sawyer started chanting the rhyme every kid hated.

"Truth or dare, double dare. Hero's act or coward's scare?"

Most kids say it as part of a game, but I could tell by the way Sawyer was trying to stare a hole right through my forehead that he was dead serious. But just like the statue of my grandfather, I would *never* blink. "Name it."

"March up to the Demons' Door and knock three times. Then we'll know there's brave blood running through your veins."

"That's c-c-crazy," Aidan said. "Ziegler's dogs'll chew you up and sp-sp-spit out your bones."

"It's okay to admit you're scared, Cory," Anne said. "Nobody cares."

She was wrong. I knew it. Aidan knew it. And most of all, Sawyer knew it. So I said the words the Space Warrior always threw into the face of danger. "I don't know the meaning of fear."

I automatically scanned the alley for the Mallory ghosts and tossed Aidan my mitt. Then I pushed my Yankees cap down to shade my eyes and stepped onto the gravel of Satan's Sidewalk. The cap from Dad became my Helmet of Power, and my steps were the Kid's fearless march of HyperSpeed Boots that left trenches in the earth behind me. Which made the fact that my knees felt like pudding a total mystery.

Anne acted like it was no big deal and fell into step beside me. Sawyer and Aidan followed, close enough to make sure I went through with the dare. It didn't help when Sawyer armed his slingshot with a walnut and shot it straight at the Demons' Door. Even though he missed, I could tell the dogs heard it crash into the bushes by the way they exploded with a spasm of snarling barks. When I started walking again, Anne fell back a few steps. I didn't blame her. Besides, a hero never wants the girl to get hurt.

The trees blocked the August sun and something rattled their leaves. Instinct made me half-duck. I didn't really expect acid dripping from a Mallory ghost to splat on my head and burn a hole clean through my brain.

Satan's Sidewalk dead-ended at the bottom of the hill. Turning right up the hill would take me to the safety of my backyard. Going straight led past the Mallory House until it emptied onto Elm Street. At the intersection of it all was Ziegler's yard and the Demons' Door. I caught glimpses of his dogs through the bushes, their gray hair tangled in the shadows. There was absolutely nothing stopping them from leaping over that puny gate and ripping my throat wide open, but heroes never turned back. They never ran. They. Knew. No. Fear.

Sawyer and Aidan slowed. Anne stopped between them and me. "D-D-Do it fast," Aidan whispered. "Before Ziegler's dogs sink their fangs down to your bones."

"Piece. Of. Cake," I said through gritted teeth.

Just ten more steps. Then five. Three more and I would be there, face-to-face with the spy's dogs. My fingers curled into a fist, ready to pound the gate hard enough for Sawyer to hear it loud and clear.

It was at that exact instant, the very moment I was going to prove Sawyer was wrong once and for all, that something crashed through the bushes of the deserted Mallory house and raced straight toward me. It was instinct, not fear, that ripped a scream from my throat.

I dodged left, but a ball of fury seemed to be everywhere, knocking against my shins and tangling my legs. I jumped back and stumbled into the strip of weeds creeping at the edge of the alley. A vine snared my shoe and pulled my feet out from under me. I butt-scooted away until I was trapped with my back against the Demons' Door, kicking for all I was worth at my attacker.

"Stop, Cory. Stop," Anne shouted. "It's only a cat."

Sure enough, when I quit kicking, I saw the mangy yellow-haired cat crouched in front of my shoes. The same one that had been hiding in the haunted house when we spied on Ziegler.

Sawyer hooted from his hidey-hole behind a trash can. "So much for the blood of the brave!"

Aidan echoed Sawyer like some bird-brained parrot. Anne stood next to both of them. All three of them eyewitnesses to how I had gotten twitchy over a silly cat. I was ready to point out that being startled was not the same thing as being scared, when something cold hit my arm and I looked up.

It wasn't acid oozing from ghosts. It was worse. Much worse.

There, with their shaggy heads hanging over the Demons' Door, were the Nazi's beasts, their lips curling over yellow teeth that turned black at the gums.

The cat hissed one last time before diving through the bushes to the Mallory yard, its tail bristling like a bottlebrush. With the cat gone, the dogs turned their gaze on me as if I were some kind of midnight sacrifice. I tried rolling away, but all that kicking had left both my shoes wrapped in vines.

"Run, Cory," Anne yelled.

"I *can't*," I said, jerking my foot as proof.

"Oh, c-c-crap," Aidan said when it finally dawned on him I was stuck.

That's when Sawyer made his move. He dove from behind the barrel, grabbed the Yankees baseball cap from my head, and tossed it over the bushes, right into the lair of the beasts. "Come and get it!" he hollered. Then he turned tail and sprinted up Satan's Sidewalk.

A rush of air chilled my sweat-soaked hair as one of the dogs snapped my imaginary Helmet of Doom out of thin air. The gate's hinges splintered when the other pushed off with an ear-splitting howl. That's when the back door flew open and the shadowy figure of Mr. Ziegler filled the doorway. "Who itz out there?"

My best friend raced after Sawyer, leaving me stranded on Satan's Sidewalk with only the rotting wood of the Demons' Door separating me from two killer hounds and the Nazi spy who commanded them.

7

THE MALLORY GHOSTS

S trength was not my superpower. I had to use every last ounce of muscle in my body to wrench the vines loose, taking a chunk of bush with them. Then I darted up Satan's Sidewalk and skidded to where Sawyer and Aidan hid in shadows. Anne should've followed me. Instead, she ran past Ziegler's and didn't stop until she reached the far side of the Mallory house.

I held my breath when Ziegler glanced our way, half-expecting him to shoot lightning bolts out of his eyes. Without my cap, I felt naked and exposed, but he turned his attention to his dogs and snapped his fingers at them. "Odin! Pandora! *Komm! Komm!*"

The dogs obeyed Ziegler so fast it left a silence as thick and heavy as blackout curtains.

"Did you see that?" I asked Sawyer once the dogs followed Ziegler inside the house. "He could've just as easily ordered them to leap that fence and tear out our throats."

"There you go again," Sawyer said. "Filling the air with Nazi spy conspiracies. All your hot air can't hide the fact that you didn't prove anything, Cory. You're nothing but a yellow-bellied chicken. Though I have to admit that seeing you run from a cat was funnier than a Marx Brothers routine."

"I'm not laughing, and I wasn't scared. I was startled. There's a difference." But as the words settled on the alley, I knew he'd never believe me. Out of habit, I reached up to pull my cap down on my head, before remembering Sawyer had just tossed it to the beasts. A new wave of anger bubbled up from my gut. "You knew that was my lucky cap."

Sawyer looked sorry for all of ten seconds. "I had to do it, Cory," he lied. "It was the only way you were going to get out of there alive."

"It was only a c-c-cap," Aidan added, sticking with Sawyer again.

Aidan knew full well Dad gave it to me when he was home on leave. "It wasn't just *any* cap."

"You c-c-could always j-j-jump the fence to get it back."

"I'd have to have one of the Warrior's StealthGrenades to try something that stupid," I snapped. "Besides, it's probably ripped to shreds by now."

The three of us glanced back down the alley at the Demons' Door. That's when we noticed Anne outside the old Mallory house. "What is this place?" she asked, her voice too light and breezy for someone who had almost been eaten by flesh-ripping devil dogs.

The two-story Victorian house had once been bright white with wooden gingerbread trim hanging from the eaves like creamy frosting on a cake. Now the shingles hung cockeyed, there was a giant hole in the roof, and most of the gingerbread trim had turned scabby with rot. The steps leading up to the back door had collapsed and the windows were nothing more than gaping holes. The sky reflecting off what was left of the broken glass made it look like the house was blinking.

"Get back here," I whisper-yelled to Anne, automatically scanning every inch of the alley for signs of acid-oozing ghosts.

"Dumb Dora," Sawyer said. "Don't you know a haunted house when you see one?" Then he walked stiffed-armed like some dead zombie back down the alley. I had to give Anne credit. She didn't flinch when Sawyer came at her.

"What makes you say it's haunted?" Anne asked, shaking free of Sawyer's zombie grip. "Have you actually seen a ghost?"

"Well, no," Aidan said. "B-B-But everybody knows the story."

"I don't," Anne said, squatting down right there in the Mallory yard. "Tell me."

"Cory tells it b-b-best," Aidan said.

Dad had told me all about the Mallorys. He'd also told me how he and Mom walked around the house on their very first date. He had stolen a kiss from my mom in the shadows of the house. Then he stole another and another. Just the thought of them getting sloppy-faced with ghosts watching was enough to make my skin get twitchy. Afterward, Dad carved their initials in the wood under the dining room window and wrapped them up with the shape of a heart. But part of the board had cracked so only half the initials were left, and dirt had caked over them.

Sawyer snorted. "Cory's too chicken the ghosts will give him nightmares to tell the story." He leaned against the crooked fencepost and Aidan moved over to stand next to him, leaving me the only one with my sneakers firmly planted outside the ghosts' territory.

I squared my shoulders and pushed past Sawyer so I could sit down with my back to a tree as if it were no big deal. Because it wasn't. It was only a stray breeze that made gooseflesh spread up my arms.

"It happened a long time ago," I said, dropping my voice low. Not because I was afraid ghosts might overhear, but because my dad always taught me to be respectful of the dead.

Anne leaned forward to catch my words.

"It was back during Prohibition times. Mr. Mallory was a deacon at the Baptist church over on Second Street, and his wife was a perfect match for him."

"F-F-Full of amens and alleluias," Aidan added.

I slapped at the tickle of a weed on my neck before continuing. "According to Mrs. Mallory, the world was headed straight to hell in a handbasket unless bootleggers and flapper girls got right with the Lord."

"D-D-Deacon Mallory preached it in the p-p-pulpit and Mrs. Mallory p-p-preached it to the women at the m-m-market."

"The rest of the town thought Mr. and Mrs. High-and-mighty should've saved the preaching for home," Sawyer said.

"How come?" Anne asked.

"Because of their daughter, that's why," Sawyer told her. "She didn't think the same way as her goody-two-shoes parents."

"Her name was Cynthia, but she w-w-went by Cyn."

The skin on my neck prickled at the mention of her name. I automatically glanced up at the old house even though I knew she wouldn't be standing in a window watching us.

"Cyn!" Anne hooted. "I bet her mother didn't like that."

A bird burst from the tree overhead and I ducked. Of course, Sawyer laughed at that. I didn't say anything, considering I was concentrating on making my heartbeat slow down to normal.

"Cyn definitely wasn't the church-going type," I continued, my voice nearing a whisper. "She didn't attend Sunday school or Wednesday night Bible study. And she definitely didn't show up at Friday night prayer services."

"I don't blame Cyn," Sawyer said. "I'd rather go where she went on Friday nights, too."

"Where was that?" Anne asked.

"Sp-Sp-Speakeasies, that's where," Aidan said.

Sawyer pretended he was loopy drunk by hiccupping. "Places full of beer and jitterbugging."

"The illegal taverns in Burlington," I explained. "Every Friday night there was a big ruckus between Cyn and her parents. Her parents would tell Cyn she had to attend church services. Cyn would refuse. All the neighbors could hear them shouting back and forth until Mr. Mallory left, stomping all the way to church. Then Cyn would march out of the house, slam the door, and catch a ride to Burlington."

A hot breeze hissed through the branches overhead, knocking a clump of dead leaves right on top of Sawyer's head. Anne giggled at that.

"It wouldn't have been so b-b-bad if the Mallorys hadn't acted like their whole f-f-family was so p-p-perfect," Aidan said.

"Gossip spread faster than chicken pox," I said with a knowing nod.

"And if there was anything Mrs. Mallory hated m-m-more than sinners, it was gossip," Aidan said. "Especially if it was about their p-p-perfect family."

Anne's mouth turned down at the corners. "I agree with Mrs. Mallory about that. People shouldn't gossip. After all, everyone has secrets."

"Oh, yeah?" Sawyer asked. "What's yours?"

A car making its way over the broken pavement of

the alley sounded like crunching bones. While we waited for it to pass, a cloud drifted overhead, smothering the yard's tangle of forsythia and thistle with shadows. Leaves shivered from a hot breath of air, and I caught a whiff of decaying garbage. Sawyer leaned toward Anne, still waiting for her answer. Anne shrugged, opened her mouth to tell us. But a shutter creaked free at that moment and banged against the Mallory house, and we all jumped. Even Sawyer. I would've ribbed him about it except I wanted to finish the story so we could get out of there.

"Mrs. Mallory decided she had to stop her daughter from bringing shame on the entire family. So one Friday night after Mr. Mallory had stomped off to church, Mrs. Mallory stood at the top of the stairs and refused to let Cyn leave."

I stopped here. If I ever let my dad down I would be a disgrace to my entire family the same way the Mallorys thought Cyn was. It wasn't a good thought.

Aidan took over the telling. "There was a f-f-fight," he said. "Cyn p-p-pushed past her mother and they both f-f-fell down the stairs."

I only jumped a little when Sawyer snapped a tree branch in two. "Broke Cyn's neck clean in half," he said. "She died at the foot of the steps. Mrs. Mallory saw what she had done and shot herself, splattering brains all over the place. When Mr. Mallory came home and found them dead, they say he went crazy on the spot. He hung himself from the attic rafters."

"J-J-Jackson says that when the moon is full you can still see his b-b-body swaying."

We automatically looked up at the small window tucked under the eaves, but nothing was there. "Ever since that day the Mallory ghosts have haunted Satan's Sidewalk, seeking revenge on gossiping people in the town," I said. "Their powers grow with each passing day, turning their ghostly essence into dripping, burning, flesh-eating acid made from pure hate and despair."

It was at that exact moment that something thumped into my back.

"AHHHHHHHHHH!" I dived onto the ground, twisting around, ready to face the vengeful ghosts. Instead, I came face-to-face with the same straw-colored cat that had attacked me before. He skittered back, clawing up a dried bunch of leaves. The cat eyed me. I eyed him.

It was Sawyer who made the first move. He slapped his knees and howled almost as loud as one of Ziegler's hounds, sending the cat skittering back into the thicket of overgrown bushes lining the Mallory yard. "That's strrrr-iiiiike three! Three times that cat has made you jump out of your breeches. Admit it, Cory. You're scared witless of that itty-bitty kitty-cat!"

I glared at him as if he were the Torch of Evil and I could zap him into oblivion with rays of annihilation from my eyeballs. At least shooting death rays would've explained why my cheeks felt like they had been singed by the Torch. "Shut up," I told him. "I'm not scared of cats and you know it."

"P-P-Prove it, Cory," Aidan said. "Truth or dare, double dare. C-C-Coward's choice or hero's scare?"

Aidan stood up just a little taller at the slow grin Sawyer gave him. "Yeah, Cory. It's time to play hardball and put your money where your mouth is. Catch that cat and stare it down, eye-to-eye and nose-to-nose, while I count to twenty."

"Catching a half-starved cat and looking it in the eyes?" I asked. "You have to be kidding. That'll be a piece of cake." Then, just because I couldn't resist, I added, "But I didn't know you could count that high."

Anne laughed so hard she snorted, which made me feel a little better. Especially since Sawyer's face spread with red all the way up to his cowlick.

Sawyer shifted his wad of gum from his right cheek to his left. "Just for that, make it fifty. Unless, of course, you really are a chicken."

"I don't know the meaning of fear."

"Yeah, yeah, yeah. We know. You're Woodford B-B-Brave," Aidan said.

I stared at Aidan. If it hadn't been for the way his tongue tripped up, I'd have sworn it was Sawyer saying it. I didn't care about the cat. He wouldn't hurt me. Except for maybe a scratch or two. Okay, so the thought of sharp claws digging into my flesh wasn't exactly appealing, but I could deal with that. No. The worst part about this dare was it had come from my best friend.

I stood, taking enough time to straighten a dog-eared page on the comic book still tucked in my hip pocket, before turning in a complete circle. "Where'd he go?"

A nod from Sawyer was all I needed to know. The cat was deep in the Mallory yard.

"You don't have to do it," Anne said matter-of-factly. "Truth or Dare is a silly game."

She was wrong, of course. If I didn't, Sawyer would tell everyone I was scared of fuzzy-wuzzy kittens and Aidan would go right along with him once and for all. "I'm not afraid of a stupid cat, and I'm not scared of ghosts," I told them. "Especially girly-ghosts."

Sawyer laughed at that, but Anne looked at me as if my words were a swarm of bumblebees between us. I reached up to tug my lucky Yankees ball cap down tight on my head, forgetting how Sawyer had fed it to the dogs. My belly flopped when I realized I was going to have to do this without my Helmet of Power. Mom always said that *hate* was a four-letter word, but at that moment I hated Sawyer for what he had done. After all, that was my lucky cap and right then, more than anything, I wanted it back.

I took one step.

Then another.

Two more steps. I willed them to become the Kid's fearless march.

I looked up at the trembling leaves, expecting ghost-acid to splash in my face and eat straight through my eyeballs. Of course, nothing was there. The three of us had been in that house before, spying on Ziegler. I knew it was all just a silly story, but telling the tale of what happened to the Mallorys made the idea of ghosts more real.

A hot breeze tickled the back of my neck and I imagined Cyn burning my skin with her breath. A bug crawling up my arm felt like a ghost clawing for veins. Even though the humid air was enough to plaster the shirt to my back, gooseflesh scattered down my neck and arms.

I paused halfway across the yard. "He's not here."

"That cat's probably halfway to Burlington by now," Anne said. "I'm going home before I'm eaten alive by chiggers." She scratched her ankles to prove it.

"Th-Th-There he is," Aidan called before I could take two steps back toward the alley.

The cat was closer to the house. He hunkered down with his ears pulled back as if he, too, heard ghosts tap-dancing on creaking floorboards. I muttered the kind of word that would've gotten my mouth washed out with soap if Mom had heard me say it, then squatted and held out my hand. The cat sniffed, pausing just long enough for me to make my move.

I snatched him by the scruff of the neck, trapping him against my chest. The cat growled, which I didn't know cats could do. Then he hissed and dug his claws into the fleshy part of my arm. I winced, but I was the Kid. I would not let go.

The cat squirmed, trying to find an escape route. When he found none, he went limp against my chest. "Start counting," I yelled to Sawyer.

"You have to g-g-get nose-to-n-n-nose."

Hearing my best friend sounding just like Sawyer stung my eyes. I imagined my grandfather checking to see if I was being Woodford Brave and bent my nose to the cat. I wondered if the ghosts of Cyn and her mother could sense fear. Not mine, of course. The cat's.

Sawyer started counting, saying each number as slow as peanut butter plops from a knife. I concentrated on the cat. Just. The. Cat.

The edge of one ear was torn completely in half and his hair was matted with burrs and grass. The darker stripe of yellow arching over his eyes gave him a worried expression. His sides rose and fell, rose and fell, rose and fell, and his tail lashing back and forth stuck to the sweat on my arm. Sawyer had only counted to eight when I noticed something hidden deep in the cat's amber eyes. It was a tiny reflection of me.

When Sawyer reached ten, Anne sneezed. It wasn't a cute little girly sneeze, either. It was the kind of sneeze that made the ground shake. The cat let out a yowl and sprang from my arms. It wasn't fear that made me dodge out of the way, but when Aidan let out a whoop that sounded just like Sawyer, I knew that he would never believe me. Sawyer wouldn't let him. Not in a million years.

Sawyer shifted his wad of gum to his left cheek as we watched the cat high-tail it around the corner of the house where Dad had once made out with Mom. "Admit it, Cory. There is no such thing as Woodford Bravery. If you ask me, that statue in the square ought to be torn down so we can have a decent baseball mound. It's nothing but a huge bird-crap catcher. Just like all your superhero stories."

I had put up with Sawyer all summer. Put up with him making fun of my baseball pitches and laughing whenever I struck out. I'd watched Aidan hang on his every word. Kept my mouth shut when he took over my place in the tree house. And he'd done the unthinkable by feeding my Yankees ball cap to a Nazi spy's dogs. This was the last straw.

Sawyer didn't know what hit him when I tackled him. He heaved, pushing me off, and I rolled to a squat, then lunged at him again. The air left his lungs with a satisfying *oomph*.

Sawyer swung. His fist connecting with the side of my face snapped my teeth through the flesh of my cheek. I jerked my head away before he could land another punch. Sweat, blood, and spit sprayed us both when I head-butted him in the chest, sending us rolling across the ground in a tangle of legs and arms. His slingshot was torn from his pocket, and I felt it dig into my back as we rolled across the gravel. We ended up with me sitting on the great high-and-mighty's chest.

"Take. It. Back," I growled, ignoring the taste of my blood.

"Stop it," Anne yelled. "Both of you."

The Kid would not stop. Woodfords never gave up. I shook Sawyer's shoulder with each word. "Say. You're. Sorry!"

Sawyer opened his mouth, but instead of apologizing, his eyes widened and his mouth started flopping open and shut like a bottom-feeder fish.

"G-G-Get off him. He's choking," Aidan yelled, grabbing me around my middle and heaving me to the ground.

Sawyer's lips were tinged blue. Anne grabbed one of his arms and Aidan grabbed the other, pulling until he was sitting up and I could pound him right between the shoulder blades. Maybe, just maybe, I hit Sawyer a little harder than I needed to, but it worked. His gum flew out of his mouth and landed in a clump of dandelions.

Did Sawyer thank the Kid for saving his life? Of course not. Instead, he gave me a look that would've curdled milk. He snatched his slingshot from the ground and stuffed it in his pocket, then grabbed his bat and mitt and stalked down the alley to Catalpa without even saying good-bye.

"What'd you go and m-m-make him mad for?" Aidan asked.

I stared at him as if he'd just started speaking German. "Me? Make HIM mad? You heard what he said about my grandfather!"

I couldn't believe the words Aidan said next. "Do us all a f-f-favor, Cory, and g-g-give that hero crap a rest." Then he jogged after Sawyer like some kind of lost puppy.

My comic book lay on the ground, the Warrior staring up at me from the torn cover. I picked it up and straightened it as best I could, acting like it didn't matter one bit that my best friend had just turned his back on me.

8

THE COURAGEOUS ADVENTURES OF THE WARRIOR KID

used my pocketknife to whittle the pencil to a sharp point, letting curls of shavings fall to the floor. I stomped on one until it was nothing but slivers. The inside of my cheek was swollen, and I was mad as a hornet at Sawyer for throwing my cap to the dogs and saying all those things about the Woodford name. But what really got to me was the way Aidan had gone along with Sawyer. Of course, I couldn't tell Dad any of it, since letters to the troops were supposed to cheer them up.

I kicked the rest of the shavings under my desk and started to write.

Dear Dad,

An old scraggly cat was hanging around the house next door to Ziegler's. He seems to be following me wherever I go. (The cat, not Ziegler.) Sawyer says the cat is worthless because he's scared of everything, but I think he's braver than he looks. (The cat, not Sawyer.) After all, he was living in the weeds right next door to Ziegler's dogs, and they're big, loud, and really mean. (The dogs, not the weeds.)

The only things Sawyer worries about are whether or not there will be a World Series or if a girl can actually hammer a nail. He's wrong about the cat being a scaredy-cat so I'm pretty sure he's wrong about the danger lurking right here in Harmony, too. I don't know why he doesn't like Anne. She seems okay to me. Although she's a little confused about Germans not being the enemy. Don't worry, I'll set her straight. Aidan, too. And don't worry one bit about Mom, either. I'm keeping her safe right along with the rest of Harmony, because I'm just like you. You and Grandpa.

WOODFORD BRAVE.

It wasn't necessary to tell Dad about not finishing the stupid dares. After all, it was the cat's fault for coming out of nowhere. That, and the fact that Anne sneezed loud enough to knock the Mallory ghosts clear to Burlington. It wasn't like I backed down or anything.

I squared off the bottom of the paper and started to sketch another courageous adventure for the Kid.

THE NEFARIOUS SPY HAD RETURNED STRONGER THAN EVER.

THE KID AND EVIL SPY WERE LOCKED IN A DUEL TO THE DEATH.

SUDDENLY, THE BOY WITH GUM BULGING IN HIS CHEEK JUMPED FROM BEHIND A BOULDER AND SNATCHED THE HELMET OF POWER.

THE KID'S POWERS FLICKERED AND THEN DRAINED INTO THE GROUND BENEATH HIS HYPERSPEED BOOTS. HE WAS DEFENSELESS AGAINST THE DOOMSDAY BEAMS SHOOTING FROM THE SPY'S GLASS EYEBALLS.

AMIDST THE CARNAGE, THE KID HEARD A FAINT WHIMPER. A FELINE CREATURE OF EPIC PROPORTIONS STALKED A HELPLESS DAMSEL. TEARS DRIBBLED FROM THE CORNERS OF HER BLUE EYES. "SAVE ME, KID. SAVE ME!"

WITHOUT HIS FATHER'S POWER FROM THE HELMET, THERE WAS NOTHING THE KID COULD DO. "I MUST FIND THE WARRIOR!" THE KID YELLED TO THE STARS. "ONLY HE CAN RESTORE MY POWER SO THAT I CAN DEFEAT THIS EVIL ONCE AND FOR ALL!"

I added a few lines, setting the Kid's face with a look of pure determination. When Dad saw my comic, he would know I was just like him. No matter what Sawyer said.

9

WHATEVER IT TAKES

"**W**ash your face," Mom said the next morning. She smoothed down my hair and gave my cheek a pat. She sounded serious, but she was smiling. "There are pencil smudges all over your forehead. I do believe more lead ends up on your face than on those cartoons of yours."

"Comics," I said. "There's a difference."

I was glad she couldn't see the way the inside of my cheek was swollen from where Sawyer had socked me. I wiped my hand across my forehead before handing her my letter. It was her day to roll bandages at the Methodist Church, so she read it fast before slipping it into the air-mail envelope.

The living room radio crackled static in time to the Glenn Miller Orchestra, but Mom had stopped listening as soon as the war report ended. "Doesn't making bandages give you the heebie-jeebies?" I asked. "Think about it. Some soldier fighting Nazis all the way over in Europe is going to need that Red Cross bandage. Somebody like Dad."

The coffee cup slipped from Mom's hand, shattering into jagged pieces by her feet. She'd used the coffee grounds so many times the water was barely tinted, but it was still hot enough to flower her ankles with burn marks.

"I didn't mean Dad," I said as I dived to the floor and started picking up the shards, but Mom tugged on my arm to stop me. "Saying Dad could get hurt is like telling the Warrior he isn't strong enough to fight the Torch of Evil."

Mom put a finger to my lips, not hard or mean, but enough to make my words stop. "I don't care if all your dad does is swab latrines, as long as he stays safe. The faster this war is over, the sooner he comes home, and I'll do whatever I can to help, whether it's rolling bandages, going without stockings, or growing radishes."

She glanced out the kitchen window at her Victory Garden when she said the last part. "Where did *that* come from?"

I pulled away from her fingers and immediately looked to the sky, expecting to see a spy plane blitzkrieging our house. But Mom wasn't looking at the sky; she had her eyes on her garden. I shoved the blackout curtains out of the way to see. There, making his way through the tomato vines, was the cat from the day before.

"He must've followed me back from the old Mallory house," I said without thinking.

"Cory!" Mom shrieked so loudly I almost dropped the pieces of her coffee cup. "I told you not to go near that place."

"We didn't go in. I was just showing Anne around the neighborhood. Don't worry. If we saw a ghost, I'd knock it clear over the moon."

"It's not ghosts I worry about," Mom said. "It's rotten floors."

She glanced out the window again and her tongue made the *tsk-tsk-tsk* that I was used to hearing whenever she disapproved of something. "It's a sin the way people dump strays, leaving them to fend for themselves. Feed him, Cory. After all, even your cartoon heroes have compassion."

"*Comic* books," I reminded her.

She kissed the top of my head and snatched her pocketbook from the counter. "Behave yourself while I'm gone." She left the kitchen, her heels click-clacking on the hardwood floor until I heard the latch of the front door closing.

I found two cracked saucers, filled one with water, and crumbled bacon in the other. As soon as he heard the squeak of the screen door, the cat zigzagged through the tomato vines like a soldier dodging enemy gunfire. He stopped at the edge of the garden, eyeing me.

"All it would take to send you straight up in the air is one stomp from the Kid's HyperSpeed Boots."

"Mrr-oww," he answered.

I was half-tempted to stomp my foot just to see how fast he would run. That's what Sawyer would've done. But the cat's nose wiggled at the dishes in my hands, and I knew for a fact he was starving, since I'd felt his ribs the day before. His eyes followed my every move until I placed the plates in a shady spot behind the garage. He waited for me to step back before wolfing down the bacon as if he hadn't eaten since the Japanese sneak-attack on Pearl Harbor nearly destroyed our navy. When he finished, he hunkered there, his pink tongue flicking over whiskers. I reached out to rub between his ears, but he pulled back with a wary look, his amber eyes locking on mine for a split second.

"Fine," I muttered. "Be that way."

I crossed the alley, figuring Aidan would be around, but Jackson told me he'd gone fishing with Sawyer. At first I thought Jackson was pulling my leg, but Jackson was dead serious.

"They went without me?"

Jackson hitched his shoulder in a shrug that made his hair curl over his collar. "Guess so. You could probably find them at Old Man Jacobs's pond."

Mr. Jacobs lived at the edge of town. He didn't mind if we used his pond as long as we shared our catch with him.

"Naw. They'll probably just catch a bunch of drowned worms, anyway." I said it as if it didn't really matter.

Without Aidan, there wasn't much to do, so I headed back across Satan's Sidewalk. The cat scooted under a bush as soon as he saw me. "I don't care if you stay, but quit acting like some big scaredy-cat. Deal?"

"Mrr-oww."

I took that as a *yes* and left the cat to nap in the safety of the shadows while I spent the afternoon alone, reading comic books.

That night, Mom stood in front of the map of Europe she'd thumbtacked to the wall and listened to the nightly radio war report. Bits of blue paper tacked to the map showed the major battles. Red paper scraps showed where Mom thought Dad might be. While her fingers traced the distances between red and blue paper, I sneaked into my parents' bedroom and opened Dad's top dresser drawer. There, neatly arranged, were the things he'd left behind: a gold pen, a pocket watch that had belonged to Grandpa, and a silver dollar.

Dad would sure as the dickens know how to convince Aidan that Sawyer was nothing but a big nincompoop. He'd tell me what to do about Ziegler, too. If only he were here so I could ask him.

I felt the edge of the silver dollar that Dad had carried in his pocket for as long as I could remember. Silver dollars were supposed to have ridges, but this one was as slick as a Buick's fender. Dad had smoothed away the letters and words, too, until both sides looked almost the same. All that was left was the faint memory of Lady Liberty's head on one side and the eagle on the other.

Dad had packed for the war as if it were nothing more than a camping trip, rubbing the coin between his thumb and finger one last time before tossing it in his drawer without a second glance. He'd given me a silver dollar once, but I'd spent it on comic books while he was at boot camp. He didn't say anything about it when he came home on leave, but I knew he was disappointed. I promised myself it wouldn't happen again. The Kid would never disappoint the Warrior. Ever.

Back in my room, I laid my comic book on the nightstand, smoothing the bent bottom corner before turning out the light. The air was thick and my sheets were soggy with sweat in no time. I parted the blackout curtains and moved the rocks lining my windowsill so I could lift out the screen.

Aidan was convinced the glittery rocks we collected when we were seven were full of diamonds that would make us rich. After Jackson told us they were worthless fool's gold, Aidan threw his rocks into Jacobs's cow pond, but I saved all of mine. Aidan's new idea of joining the Majors was just another get-rich-quick plan, and that's why he was hanging onto Sawyer's shirttails. Still. Best friends should never turn their backs on each other. It was obvious that I'd have to prove Sawyer was full of beans to get Aidan to come to his senses.

It was so hot I wouldn't have minded if Cyn Mallory herself had popped in front of me and blown the sweat off my face. I leaned on the sill, resting my head on my arms. I could've sworn I heard the ghosts singing a mournful song at the bottom of Satan's Sidewalk, but I convinced myself that it was nothing more than the creak of an old tree. The place where the cat had scratched me stung when I picked off part of the scab.

The branches of the maple tree outside my window blurred as I imagined being the Kid, wearing a cape the color of a ripe plum, fighting side by side with my dad. He'd be the Warrior and I'd be his sidekick. Together, we'd bat planes from the sky as if they were just pesky mosquitoes. Nothing could scare the Hero and his Kid. Not rumbling tanks or buzzing planes. Not stuttering machine guns or even the blinding flashes of grenades. We'd be invincible.

Ziegler's dogs split the night with an outburst of barks, reminding me where I was.

If only Dad were here, we'd knock those dogs' heads together, leaving them on the ground with little stars floating around their limp ears. Then we'd capture Ziegler single-handedly before ridding Satan's Sidewalk of the Mallory ghosts once and for all. My cape would billow in the wind, its fabric fortified to withstand anything the Mallory ghosts lobbed my way.

Thanks to us, the alleys of Harmony would be safe for helpless kids like Anne. Aidan and Sawyer, too. Of course, just like the Space Warrior, we would never take credit, since the safety of the people would be the only reward we needed.

Although a medal would be nice. One that I could pin to my cape.

I was imagining my hero's ceremony when a shadow

hurtled across the tree branches right in front of my face. I fell back, butt-scooting across the floor as something leaped through my open window, landed on the sill, and thumped to the floor all in one fluid movement. I sucked in hot air until my heart regained an even beat and I could snap on my lamp.

I don't know who was more surprised. Me—or the huffing yellow cat. A flick of his tail sent a tumbleweed of matted hair under my bed. "Sawyer said you were nothing but a dumb cat, but you figured out how to climb up here and jump in my window, so you can't be all that stupid. I bet you're smarter than he is."

The cat's ears flicked forward to catch my words, then went back again.

"Okay, okay. Sometimes it's hard to tell who's a friend and who's not, but you have to stop sneaking up on me, okay?"

This time he answered with a deep-throated "Mrr-oww."

I held out a hand and watched his ears twitch forward as he eyed my fingers. He took a step in my direction, but kept his belly low to the ground like a soldier crawling under the barbed wire of a battlefield. He took his time closing the space between us, his tail slowing from wild lashing to a lazy swish. I reached out to rub the spot between his ears where the darker orange coloring made a letter *M*. He tensed at my touch, but then relaxed and lifted his head so I could rub harder.

His fur was matted under his chin and on his belly. Leaves were caught in the bushy hair of his tail. To fill the quiet space of night, I told him about Dad as I picked out the burrs and tangles. Whenever I paused the cat echoed with a "Mrr-oww."

"He's like Grandpa. A hero."

"Mrr-oww."

"And I'm going to be just like both of them."

"Mrr-oww."

"I call myself the Kid. Nothing scares me."

"Mrr-oww?"

I knew the cat couldn't really understand what I was saying, but it made me a little mad that his meow sounded more like a question just then.

"You did *not* scare me when we were in the Mallory yard. I was just surprised when you bumped into me, that's all."

"Mrr-oww."

Then I told him exactly how I planned to battle the Nazi spy at the bottom of Satan's Sidewalk. Just like a superhero would. By the time I finished, his hair was smooth and soft. "You can stay," I whispered. "You could be my sidekick. Since you have something to say about everything, your name could be Echo."

But this time he didn't answer. The Mighty Echo was already asleep.

10

BATTLE LINES

"I'm pretty sure the Space Warrior never had to sweep out his neighbor's garage," I said the next morning.

"It won't hurt you to help out a neighbor," Mom said. "Now scoot."

Altering time obviously wasn't my superpower, because the minutes dragged by while I worked in Mrs. Springgate's garage. When I moved the boxes to a corner so they'd be out of the way, I found a wagon jammed against a wall. Two boxes inside the wagon were neatly packed with a child's clothes. A teddy bear with a missing eye and torn nose was on top of one box.

For as long as I could remember, Mrs. Springgate had been just the old lady who lived next door. I knew her husband had died before I was even born, but these boxes revealed a past that included a little boy who once carried a teddy bear until its eye fell off. Since Mom and Dad had never mentioned him, I figured it could only mean one thing. Mrs. Springgate's son was dead just like her husband. The fact that Mrs. Springgate sat on her porch drinking beer made a little more sense.

I replaced the teddy bear and stacked the boxes in the wagon. I was a little irritated when Echo jumped onto a pile of old clothes for a nap, as if he didn't have a care in the world, while I hoisted the other boxes into a neat stack. "Good-for-nothing lazy bum."

Thunk.

I glanced across the alley. Anne was in her backyard, shooting rocks at a target propped against the garage. Anne had said we were knuckleheads to think Ziegler was a spy just because he was German. I'd have to set her straight about that. Everyone knew the Germans were our enemy.

Thunk.

Anne sure didn't look like a damsel in distress, the way she squared her shoulders and sent rocks smashing into the bull's-eye. She was a good shot. Much better than Sawyer, though he'd never admit it.

The thought of Sawyer and Aidan sitting in the tree house, going fishing, and working together to make their own slingshots really rankled. As soon as Dad got home, I'd make a slingshot that would send Sawyer all the way to the Torch of Evil's planet. I tried to ignore how swollen the inside of my cheek was from where Sawyer had socked me a good one. At least Sawyer's elbow was scraped raw and he had lost that wad of gum he'd been working over for the last two weeks.

Thunk.

A spider web stretched across one corner of the garage. "I ought to be figuring out how to capture Ziegler instead of fighting spider webs," I mumbled to Echo, who didn't even twitch a whisker to help.

I imagined being the Kid, accompanied by a trusted feline sidekick. Armed with my broom of annihilation, I batted down webs formed by giant acid-injected zombie spiders planning to suck my super-warrior blood dry and use it for nefarious purposes. I was attacking a web that had attached itself to my leg when Aidan interrupted my daydream.

"Nice d-d-dance."

The clatter my broom made when I dropped it sent the cat flying out the door. So much for being my fearless sidekick.

Sawyer and Aidan stood side by side. It hadn't taken Sawyer long to replace the wad of gum that had almost killed him. A bruise the size of a chicken egg jumped when Sawyer switched the wad from his left cheek to his right. His bat rested on his shoulder, his mitt dangling from the tip, and he carried his new slingshot in his hip pocket the way I carried my comic books.

I picked up the broom and tried sweeping the spider web off my leg, making sure nothing with eight legs was crawling for higher ground.

"Mom said to tell you I'm sorry," Sawyer mumbled around the gum, but I could tell he didn't mean it by the way he kept his eyes narrowed. "She said I shouldn't have said all those things. I guess I did sort of throw you a curveball. You still sore at me?"

I reached up to adjust my cap, forgetting yet again that it was gone. As long as I'd been wearing it, I'd felt like Dad and I were a team. But now that link was gone. It made me want to sweep Sawyer's head right off his neck. But Jackson was shuffling across the alley and I was pretty sure Aidan's brother would tell on me if I tried to behead another kid.

"Naw. I guess not," I lied.

Jackson stepped into the shade of Mrs. Springgate's garage and leaned against the wall.

"Then let's p-p-play ball," Aidan shouted, loud enough to send Ziegler's dogs into a barking frenzy.

"I have to finish this first. Mom's making me."

"What're you doing?" Sawyer asked.

I looked at the broom. The garage floor. The pile of dirt by my feet. Back at Sawyer. I knew he wasn't the smartest kid in Harmony, but that had to be the stupidest question to ever make it past his wad of gum. "Um . . . sweeping."

Sawyer rolled his eyes. "I know *that*. But sweeping's a girl's job. Why are *you* doing it?"

The *thunk*ing stopped and Anne leaned over her fence, trying to hear every word.

"I'll do it," Jackson said. Obviously, Jackson was not embarrassed to do what Sawyer called girls' work. I glared at Sawyer, waiting for him to razz Jackson like he had me, but all he did was shift his gum to the other cheek.

"Thanks, J-J-Jackson," Aidan said. Then he gave me a shove. "Cory owes you one. He'll have to hurry to repay you before you l-l-leave for the Marines."

Great. Jackson would probably think of something worse than sweeping out a dusty garage. It didn't make me feel any better when Echo wrapped his body between Jackson's ankles.

"I'll remember that," Jackson said, then reached down and scratched my cat's ears. "Now get lost."

"I'll get my mitt," Anne hollered from across the alley.

"Forget it," Sawyer said before she got two steps from her gate. "Baseball isn't for girls, right, Aidan?"

"R-R-Right," Aidan said. "The M-M-Majors don't allow girls, so neither do we."

"Tell that to the Peaches," Jackson said. "They're part of League play now."

That sure took me by surprise since I figured Jackson would follow only the men's league.

Sawyer didn't bat an eyelash. "Well, there are no Peaches in Harmony," he said. "Are you on our team, Cory? Or are you going to stay here and play house with your girlfriend?"

"She's not my girlfriend," I muttered.

"Then you're w-w-with us," Aidan said.

It was as obvious as the shadow stretching from my grandfather's statue that Sawyer had drawn a battle line smack dab down the middle of Satan's Sidewalk, with Anne on one side and us on the other. Just like the Americans against the Nazis or the Space Warrior versus the Torch of Evil. Being on any side with Sawyer made me feel like I had bitten into a rotten apple, but what choice did I have? Aidan was my best friend. Of course I had to side with him.

Once the three of us got to the square, Sawyer made every pitch and every swing of his bat look effortless. When I was up to bat I felt like my muscles and joints were made of broken rubber bands. It didn't help that every time I reached up to adjust my cap, my hand grabbed nothing but hair. It was Sawyer's fault that cap was gone, which made me want to hit a ball straight at Sawyer's grinning face. But of course, all I ended up hitting was air.

I had to admit that Sawyer was acting extra nice by yelling out pointers and not throwing a beanball even once. Still, I was glad when Mr. Franklin stepped outside the Drug Emporium and shouted to me.

"The new books are in, Cory. I saved a Space Warrior for you!"

It used to be that Aidan would race me to buy the latest edition first, but now I wasn't sure he'd want to come. "I'm going to go check it out. How about you?"

"Sure, Cory," Aidan said, making me feel a little better. Then he ruined it. "Won't we, Sawyer?"

"Pretty soon you're going to need Sawyer's permission to pee," I muttered, turning to push open the door to Franklin's. The drugstore felt like a cave after being out in the sun, mostly because Mr. Franklin had plastered the windows with posters advertising defense saving stamps, war bonds, and the government's price control order. I slowed, letting my eyes adjust.

Mr. Franklin looked over the drug counter at us. Ever since Aidan and I knocked down an entire display of citrate of magnesia, he always watched to make sure we weren't goofing off when we came into his store. I was extra-careful to walk around the pyramid of Gold Medal Flour and Quaker Oats that he'd built by the front door.

The store's wood floors were scratched and warped, and the windows were grimy with dust. The front of the store was filled with shelves of girly things like face powder and lipstick. We headed to the back, where Mr. Franklin kept the comic books. With paper getting scarce because of the war effort, he only ordered the most popular ones. Most of them showed superheroes like Captain America, the Boy Commandos, and Superman battling Hitler and his evil axis of power. But Mr. Franklin always stocked the Mighty Space Warrior for me.

Sawyer picked up the latest issue of the Young Allies. "There ought to be a comic book about baseball players. I can't believe you still read this junk, Cory."

He'd never liked comic books, so I was used to him making fun of the Space Warrior, but I never expected Aidan to say what he said next. "Cory does more than read about the Space Warrior. He p-p-pretends to be him."

Sawyer hooted at that. "What do you do? Tie your mom's bathrobe around your neck and try to fly? Or do you wear your underwear over your trousers and leap off Mrs. Springgate's garage?"

"Gee, Aidan. With friends like you, who needs enemies?" I asked.

"I d-d-didn't mean anything by it," Aidan said.

"We're just pulling your leg," Sawyer said, play-punching my arm and obviously trying to make nice. Then he reached into his pocket and pulled out a penny. "Here, I found this. You can put it toward your comic book."

"Your copy's on the shelf," Mr. Franklin hollered from where he was stacking soap powder. "Right next to the laxatives."

"That man gives me the creeps," Sawyer said.

"Why?" Aidan asked.

"That, for one thing," he said, pointing to the fetal pig floating in a jar of formaldehyde on a shelf next to a collection of amber-colored apothecary bottles, a broken brass scale, and a marble pestle and mortar. The jar had been there so long the glass was grimy and dust coated the lid. The pig was curled up, its hind legs tucked under its snout so you couldn't see the umbilical cord. Its eyes were shut, but not squeezed tight, and it wore a faint smile as though a funny thought had flitted through its tiny brain. I wondered if the pig had been dreaming at the moment it died and if the dream was imprinted on its brain, stuck there for all eternity. It was sort of sad to think it would never get the chance to do all the piggy things that pigs usually do.

Sawyer jabbed me in the side. "Better watch out so that Franklin doesn't stuff you in a jar and pickle you forever."

"Maybe he's like Dr. F-F-Frankenstein," Aidan whispered. "Their names even sound alike, and the p-p-pig could be one of his experiments!"

"Isn't Frankenstein a *German* name?" Sawyer asked. "Maybe he changed it to Franklin."

"J-J-Jackson said lots of Germans changed their names to sound more American. It's been on the radio and in all the newspapers."

That was true. Mom said people did it during the Great War, too. I looked at Mr. Franklin. He did look sort of shifty, the way his eyes roved around the store and his hands kept touching things. First a bottle of alcohol. Then a box of bandages. Darting here and there.

"He can't be a spy," Sawyer said. "He's lived in Harmony forever."

"Heinck worked in America for thirteen years as a toolmaker," I reminded him. "Before he was caught and tried as a Nazi spy."

We'd all heard the story of the eight Nazi spies who landed submarines on American soil. Most, including Heinck, had spent time in the United States before coming back to blow up places that made materials for the war against Germany. They were caught before they got a chance, but it didn't mean there weren't more spies just like them hiding in plain sight.

Sawyer sucker-punched me in the gut. It was a light punch, but it was still enough to make me gulp air. "Hey, Cory," he said, his voice full of sarcasm. "If you're so brave, why don't you go ask him if he's part of the same ring as Ziegler?"

"I already proved how brave I am," I reminded him, hearing my own voice getting snappy.

"Nuh-uh," Sawyer said. Then he started counting things up on his fingers. "You didn't prove Ziegler was a spy, you didn't knock on the Demons' Door, and you dropped that cat so fast I'm surprised sparks didn't fly off your fingertips."

"He's r-r-right," Aidan said. "You didn't prove anything."

I had a twitchy urge to push both of them right into the display of Morton's Salt. But the bells over the door jingled and Sawyer stood on tiptoes to try to see over the shelf of shampoo.

"This could be a rendezvous with another spy happening right under our noses," Sawyer said, dropping his words to a whisper. "What are you going to do about it, Cory? Hide behind the salt or go get 'em?"

Woodfords never hid and they never ran. I stepped around the tower of salt, half-expecting a Nazi to be aiming a gun at my heart. But it was only Anne. Mr. Franklin smiled when he saw her. "There you are," he said, not sounding a bit like a spy. "I found something in my cellar you can have for your project. It's in the alley for you."

"Thanks, Mr. Franklin," Anne said. She glanced back at the three of us peeking around the shelf. She eyeballed the jar of formaldehyde before looking straight at me.

"Nice pig," she said. Then she turned and walked out the front door.

"Wh-Wh-What's *she* up to?" Aidan asked.

"I'll find out," I said, knowing full well Aidan would leave Sawyer behind to follow me.

Aidan gave me a grin. A real one. "Now you're t-t-talking."

I shoved in front of Sawyer and went out the door in super-stealth mode. Hugging the side of the store, I kept my back flat to the rough bricks and led the way around the building. Slowly. Quietly. I peeked around the corner to the alley. Anne was tugging on a plank of plywood almost as big as she was.

"What are you doing?" Sawyer blurted. The Space Warrior would've cringed at the way he blew our cover.

Anne turned, hands on her hips, and glared at us. "That's for me to know and you to find out."

"We'll help you lug it home if you tell us," Sawyer bartered.

"I don't need your help or anyone else's."

"Yes, you do," Sawyer said. "Girls are weaklings. They can't carry heavy stuff like lumber."

"Just watch."

It took a few tries, but Anne hoisted the plywood up on her head, and after a few wobbly steps she was able to carry that piece of wood the entire three blocks back to Satan's Sidewalk. Of course we followed. Aidan carried the bat and mitts so Sawyer could fire rocks at the board with his slingshot. I was glad that every one of his rocks missed. We all took turns throwing guesses about what she was planning.

"Is it a bookshelf?"

"A t-t-toy box?"

"A dollhouse?"

Anne acted as though our words were nothing more than wind whispering through leaves. Once she stepped foot onto Satan's Sidewalk, I automatically became the Kid, checking tree branches for signs of the Mallory ghosts. I was ready to protect a damsel in distress even though Anne really didn't fit the description of any damsels in stories I had read. Ziegler's dogs started barking as soon as our feet hit the alley, but that didn't slow down Anne.

"I'm heading home," Sawyer said. "I've had enough of this."

Anne had obviously gotten under his skin by proving he was wrong about the way girls should act. I figured he didn't want to walk past Ziegler's dogs, either. I wasn't sorry to see him go.

Aidan and I kept after Anne. "Come on, you can tell us," I said, but my words only bounced off her back as if

91

she were surrounded by a shield of invincibility. Without saying good-bye, Anne turned into the Burkes' garage and dumped the plank on the floor with a big *smack*.

Most kids would've hurled a few insults our way, or at least thumbed their noses. Not Anne. She acted like we didn't even exist. For some reason, that made it even worse when she grabbed the cord and pulled the garage door shut.

11

SUCKER PUNCH

nne worked in her garage for the next three days. The only time she left was to take her dad a sack lunch down at the hardware store. "We'll spy on her from our tree house," I decided.

It rankled me right down to my toenails when Aidan and Sawyer grabbed the platform and left me to perch in the branches. They sat there side by side, aiming their slingshots at any bird or squirrel stupid enough to wander by. At least they missed every single time, or else I would've felt bad.

There was no way I could see inside Anne's garage from my vantage point. Not even with Grandpa's old binoculars. I checked out Satan's Sidewalk while Aidan and Sawyer went on and on about the Yankees's batting averages as if they were secret codes.

Doris Day singing to Les Brown's Orchestra floated across Satan's Sidewalk from Mom's radio, colliding with Jackson's station playing Sinatra. Mrs. Springgate sat on her back stoop, sipping beer from a mason jar. My cat hung out at the base of the tree for a while. He'd been sneaking into my room every night and this morning I'd woken with him sprawled across my belly. I was getting used to having him around. He rubbed his head on the tree bark right below where I swung my feet until he got bored and went wandering. I knew when he reached the end of the alley because Ziegler's dogs let loose with a volley of barks.

"They smell that cat's fear," Sawyer said.

"Who says Echo's scared?" I asked.

"It's a cat. Everyone knows how jumpy they are. That cat's even the color of fear. Yellow."

"He ought to be scared. Those dogs c-c-could tear him apart in ten seconds flat," Aidan said.

"Ziegler's dogs could tear anyone apart," I pointed out. "He probably plans to use them to help the Nazis take over Harmony."

"The Nazis can have this sorry excuse for a town as far as I'm concerned," Sawyer said. "Just as soon as I join a Major League team."

I was ready to remind him that fighting Nazi aggression was more important than baseball, but Anne's grandmother pushed open the back door. The screen door bumped against her hip and she held a crumpled sack in her hand. We knew what was in the sack. Her father's lunch.

"Anya?" she yelled toward the garage.

"Anya?" Sawyer repeated in a whisper.

Anne skipped out of the garage, clapping her hands free of dust. She snatched the lunch from her grandmother and headed around her house and down the street toward the hardware store. She did everything just as she had the last two days, except for one thing. She left the garage door open.

I jumped from that tree faster than my cat could pounce on a rat. Sawyer and Aidan almost fell out of the tree when they realized what my mission was. They acted like it was a race to the death, but there was no way they could catch up. Echo appeared from a clump of bushes and frisked at my heels, stopping when I reached the shadows of Anne's garage.

I paused, letting my eyes adjust to what light struggled through the single grimy window over a workbench. When I figured out what Anne was building in the middle of the floor, I laughed loud enough to make the cat meow.

Sawyer shoved me aside so he and Aidan could see.

Aidan let out a whistle. "Would you l-l-look at that?"

"I never would've guessed it," Sawyer said, snorting as if dust had flown up his nose. "Not from a *girl*."

A space in the middle of the garage was swept clean. The plywood was sanded and painted the same color as the shutters of her house. One two-by-four was secured to the plywood at the back with several eyebolts. Another two-by-four was connected to the front of the wooden plank with a single eyebolt in the center, allowing it to pivot for steering. At the ends of the two-by-fours were wheels from an old baby carriage.

I walked around the crude go-cart, running my finger along its smooth wood and testing the tightness of the bolts. The design was simple but it worked. "She said she wanted to build things," I said. "She wasn't lying. She only needs to tie a rope to the ends of the front two-by-four to use for steering. Anne's done a good job."

"Not as good as I could."

Sawyer was bragging that he was better at something he'd never even tried. It galled me to the core, and it didn't help that Aidan was eating it up like penny candy.

"But *you* didn't build a go-cart," I said. "Anne did."

Every ounce of friendliness drained out of Sawyer faster than beer from one of Mrs. Springgate's jars. "Are you implying that a *girl* is better than me, Cory?"

"You're the one always spouting off that actions speak louder than words. So, yeah. Anne proved she *is* better than you by actually building a go-cart." I should've stopped right there, but I just couldn't let it go. "This proves she's better at building things just like she proved she's better than you at *baseball*."

Aidan sucked in a breath while Sawyer eyed me as if I'd just declared war on the Major Leagues. He shifted his wad of gum to the other cheek, then spat at the rear wheel of Anne's go-cart. "You daring me to prove you wrong, Cory?"

"Just calling it like I see it," I said.

"Get this straight, Cory. A dumb Dora like Anne is not better than *me*. At anything." His teeth were gritted and I figured it was taking all his willpower to keep from throttling me. "If it's proof you want, Cory, then it's proof you'll get. You with me, Aidan?"

For a split second, I was confused. Then it hit me like a sucker punch from one of Sawyer's infamous beanballs. They were planning to build a go-cart. Just the two of them.

Well, Aidan could go ahead and help Sawyer. I'd build one of my own, too. One that was better than Sawyer's and Anne's combined. Then Aidan would be sorry. Sorry that he chose Sawyer over me.

I spent the rest of the afternoon doodling designs for a cart that would make the Space Warrior proud. Of course, there was no way mine could really have airplane boosters or armored panels, but I liked thinking about how jealous Sawyer and Aidan would be if it could.

Echo was sprawled on my chest the next morning. As soon as he saw my eyes open, he stood up, stretched, and meowed that it was about time I got up.

Mom was in the kitchen, sitting at the table. The static on the radio blended with the coffee bubbling in the percolator. Mom said she didn't care about music, that she only kept the radio on in case there was an important news bulletin. But I noticed that her shoe was keeping time to Glenn Miller's "Chattanooga Choo-Choo" while she went through a pile of Dad's letters spread out on the table. They had all come the day before in one big bundle. "He says he misses my meatloaf," Mom said. "I wonder if he's getting enough to eat?"

Her question made me feel guilty about the cornflakes in my bowl.

"This one mentions your cartoons."

"They're *comics*, Mom."

Mom looked up and smiled. "Your dad said they made him laugh. Isn't that what cartoons do?"

"*The Adventures of The Warrior Kid* isn't supposed to be funny. He's battling evil. Just like Dad," I told her. "And just like the Warrior, I bet Dad is beating the Germans single-handedly."

Mom's smile tightened into a scowl. "I hope you're wrong, Cory. All I want is for him to turn and run away. Run as fast as he can."

I nearly blew milk out my nose. "This is Dad you're talking about," I reminded her.

"I know that, Cory. And I'd rather he was safe instead of trying to prove he's some kind of hero."

Her words made no sense to me. "Dad's a Woodford and Woodfords are just like the Space Warrior. We never run."

I left Mom sitting at the kitchen table, searching for hidden messages written between lines.

My grandfather's stony stare followed me across the square on my way to the hardware store. The sun was hot on my head. I got mad every time I thought of Sawyer throwing my cap to Ziegler's dogs. As soon as Dad came home, he was probably going to ask why I didn't just jump the fence and get it back. "It's not that I was scared," I muttered to Grandpa's unblinking eyes. "It would've been a waste of effort to even try to get it back. Those dogs already had it in their jaws of death."

Mr. Franklin was sweeping the sidewalk in front of the Drug Emporium. Keeping a fetal pig floating forever in a jar was suspicious, even for someone who collected old medical paraphernalia. Maybe Franklin was some kind of Nazi scientist. That would explain why Ziegler moved to Harmony in the first place. What better place than a town like Harmony to work on a secret weapon with an evil scientist? I'd have to keep an eye out for Franklin and Ziegler both.

Anne's father was weighing nails for a customer when I got to Nichols's Hardware. Mr. Burke was a little on the dumpy side and had a bald spot on the back of his head. He wore glasses that kept sliding down low on his nose. I didn't think he looked a bit like Anne, but then people were always saying I was the spitting image of my dad and all I saw when I looked in the mirror was a skinny kid with a cowlick. By the time I found the eyebolts and a few other things I was going to need for my go-cart, Mr. Nichols had come out of the back room and traded places with Anne's father. I never got a chance to talk to Mr. Burke.

Hot air slapped me in the face when I went back outside.

I squinted from the glare of the sun, missing my cap more than ever as I headed up Catalpa and past Aidan's house. I knew the grain elevator dumped planks of wood out back. It was just down the street from the VFW so I could check there, too. The alley behind the VFW almost always had a wall of wooden booze crates.

It was nearly noon before I had everything piled on Dad's workbench in our garage, and sweat covered every square inch of my body. Aidan's garage was closed tighter than a jar of Mom's stewed tomatoes, but I knew he and Sawyer were in there because something crashed and I heard one of them laugh. I couldn't tell whether it was Aidan or Sawyer. They were starting to sound like identical twins.

"I don't care," I told the cat, who settled near me on a pile of rags. "Not. One. Bit."

I was getting used to how he echoed everything I said with a deep-throated *mrr-oww* of his own.

I stacked everything on the workbench and then took out the sketch I'd scribbled the night before. My go-cart would have high sides, like a tank. When I closed my eyes I could see it unfold like panels in a comic book. Echo would be my mighty sidekick as we sped down Satan's Sidewalk in the Kid's Tank of Destruction. Solid and sturdy, barreling through a ghost ambush, we'd run down a fleeing troop of Nazi spies while bombs exploded all around us.

"Building something, I see."

Mrs. Springgate's voice snapped me out of my daydream so fast I dropped my pencil. It scared Echo, too. He didn't look very mighty when he dove behind a box full of Grandpa's old books.

"Yes, ma'am," I said. Which sounded a lot more polite than how I felt.

Mrs. Springgate stood in the open garage door, a paper bag full of trash hugged to her chest. She wore a dirty dress without stockings. Most women didn't wear them anymore, considering silk was needed for parachutes, but stockings would've done wonders to cover the blue veins crisscrossing her calves. So would a hat, to hold down the tufts of gray hair sticking up all over her head.

"You're like your grandfather."

"Yes, ma'am, and if the war's still on when I'm eighteen, I'll ship out just like Dad. Woodfords are always ready to battle archenemies."

Mrs. Springgate blew a puff of air through her teeth. "*Pffft.* I'm not talking about the war. I meant building things."

I blinked. I didn't follow her.

"*Building things*," Mrs. Springgate said a little louder, as if I were deaf. "Your grandfather built things."

"He did?"

Mrs. Springgate plopped the bag of garbage on the ground. "Of course he did. Just look at all the tools."

"These are *Dad's*," I told Mrs. Springgate.

"Now they are, but they were your grandfather's to

begin with. He was a builder, that man. Spent hours in this garage, hammering and sanding. Had a real knack. Not like your dad. Your father didn't have the patience or the vision. Couldn't see inside the wood like your grandfather did." Mrs. Springgate tapped her temple three times by her right eye.

Dad had always organized his tools. Kept them wiped clean and in neat lines on the wall. But now that she brought it up, I didn't remember a single time Dad did anything more than hammer nails in the walls to hang pictures. Evidently Grandpa did. Anne had asked what kind of man my grandfather was; now I had something to tell her. She'd probably like that, considering she was pretty handy with a hammer, too.

"So, tell me about it," Mrs. Springgate said.

I blinked at her again.

"That thing you're building."

"A cart," I stammered. "A go-cart. If I can find everything I need."

Mrs. Springgate looked like she was chewing on her tongue. "Like in those Soap Box Derbies? Follow me." She turned around just as fast as she changed topics, and started walking down the alley. "Well, come on. And put that in the trash barrel on your way."

Echo sailed over the box of rags and nearly tripped me in his hurry to beat us into Mrs. Springgate's garage. She glanced at the piles of boxes and crates that I'd spent most of a day organizing. "Should be plenty in here you can use," she said. "Whatever you find is yours as long as you clean up after you dig through it."

The idea was almost too good to be true. "I can have *anything?*"

Mrs. Springgate was almost out the garage door, but she paused and I saw her face soften. "I know how boys like to build things," she said, making me think of that box full of kids' toys I'd put in the wagon. Then she looked at Echo weaving around my ankles. "Found a mouse's head on my back porch this morning. Your cat's a good mouser."

And then Mrs. Springgate walked back up the crumbling sidewalk, leaving me surrounded by a lifetime of junk. I looked at Echo. He was casually licking a paw and using it to wash behind his ears. "You? A mouser?"

For once, he didn't answer. Instead, he turned his back so all I saw was his tail swishing across the floor of Mrs. Springgate's garage.

The right side of the garage was full of Mr. Springgate's things. There was an old rifle that I knew Mom would never let me have. An axe covered in rust. Some overalls and plaid shirts. Toward the front of the garage, near the door, were paint cans. Some still sloshed. I piled what I thought I could use into the wagon and carted it home, pausing right outside Aidan's garage.

I heard Sawyer and Aidan having a grand ol' time in there.

"Aidan. Is. MY. Friend," I said, kicking a wagon wheel. I wiped my eyes. It was sweat, not tears. The Kid never cried. Ever.

Then I rolled the wagon inside my garage to work on my go-cart with no one for company but a stray cat and the ghosts of Satan's Sidewalk.

THE COURAGEOUS ADVENTURES OF THE WARRIOR KID AND HIS SIDEKICK

12

Dear Dad,

Boy, Sawyer sure was steamed when Anne struck him out. He can't get over the idea that a girl is better than him at anything— especially baseball. Serves him right since he acts like he knows everything, but I set him straight. Yes sir- ee. You would've been proud of me when I made him eat a huge serving of Woodford humble pie.

I still don't understand why Aidan doesn't get what a blowhard Sawyer is. Just because Sawyer can hit a baseball doesn't mean he's better than everyone. Afterall, he can't hit the broadside of a garage with that slingshot he made. I was going to make a slingshot, too, but decided to wait for you so we can make one that Sawyer will be jealous of.

I cut pictures of Nazi war planes off the backs of cereal boxes and hung them on my bedroom wall right over my desk. I study them every night so I'll be ready in case one flies over Harmony. Sawyer

105

said it's a waste of time, but I reminded him that Germans are everywhere. There are even rumors that America was invaded by U-boats that landed right on the coasts of Long Island and Florida. Don't worry, though. I'm keeping Harmony safe until you get home. I told the new girl about the Mallory Ghosts today, but I know we don't really have to worry about ghosts so I'm not scared. Not even a little bit.

I knew if Dad were here he'd tell me Anne was full of pinto beans; that being German was the same as being a Nazi and that spies could be tall and skinny and wear wire glasses that sat crooked on their noses just like Ziegler. Instead, I squared off the rest of the paper, sharpened my pencil, and started to draw the continuing adventure of the Kid.

ALL SEEMED LOST UNTIL, SUDDENLY, THE MONSTROUS FELINE LUNGED THROUGH
THE SMOLDERING WRECKAGE AND LANDED BETWEEN THE KID AND HIS ARCHENEMY.

THE KID PREPARED TO BATTLE
THE GIANT CAT, BUT THE DAMSEL
CRIED OUT A WARNING.

"NO, KID! NO! IT'S NOT WHAT YOU THINK."

FOR THE FIRST TIME IN THE HISTORY OF THE UNIVERSE, THE KID FALTERED. IT WAS ONLY A SPLIT SECOND, BUT IT WAS LONG ENOUGH FOR HIM TO SEE A QUESTION CLOUDING HIS MIND.

COULD THE DAMSEL BE RIGHT?

THE CAT WASN'T AN ENEMY AT ALL. HE WAS A VICTIM TANGLED IN A BURNING NET. SOMETHING BURIED DEEP WITHIN THE KID'S CHEST PINGED. HE CAST A NET OF INVINCIBILITY OVER BOTH OF THEM AND SET TO WORK FREEING THE FELINE FROM THE EVIL SPY'S WICKED KNOTS. THE SPY THREW EVERYTHING IN HIS ARSENAL. THE KID'S NET OF INVINCIBILITY WEAKENED WITH EACH ATTACK.

THAWK!

SIZZLE!

THE KID DIDN'T STOP UNTIL THE CAT WAS FREED FROM THE SPY'S NET. HE PAUSED LONG ENOUGH TO LOOK INTO THE AMBER EYES OF THE FELINE BEFORE THEY BOTH TURNED TO FACE THE ENEMY.

NOW THAT THE KID DID NOT STAND ALONE, A NEW BURNING ENERGY BUBBLED FROM DEEP WITHIN HIM.

"I don't need a best friend, because I have you for my sidekick," I told the cat. "You're the Mighty Echo. Together, we're invincible."

Echo reached out and snagged my pencil with one of his claws, but he didn't mean anything by it. I could tell from his rumbling purr.

13

GUILTY BY ASSOCIATION

It took two days to collect everything I needed. I half-expected Aidan to mosey over and tell me I could join them, but Aidan and Sawyer kept the garage locked up tighter than a mummy's coffin. Other than when Mom brought me peanut butter sandwiches and milk, Echo was my only company. He curled his tail around his paws and paid attention as if he might try building a go-cart himself. Telling him what I was doing helped fill the silence. "I'll use a crate for the body of my cart."

True to his name, Echo answered each of my comments with a comment of his own.

"It's the wheels that I still need. Most people already donated old tires for the war effort."

"Mrr-oww."

"I'll have to look hard to find four that match."

"Mrr-oww."

"The Germans have ruined everything, haven't they?" Jackson said, interrupting my conversation with Echo.

"Because of them, a kid like you has a hard time finding tires for a go-cart."

Aidan's brother leaned against the garage doorframe, half in the sunlight and half in shadow. His hair was longer, combed back in a ducktail style. Of course, that would be gone by the end of the month when he headed for boot camp. I felt my face burn. Here he was getting ready to go fight in a war, and I was worrying about wheels for what amounted to nothing more than a toy.

Jackson walked over to the bench and picked up my sketch. "Sawyer's design isn't as good as this."

"Thanks," I said, unable to hide my smug grin.

He put down the sketch and picked up a hammer, testing the weight by tossing it from his right hand to his left. It smacked his palm when he caught it. "Try using wagon wheels. That's what Sawyer and Aidan are using."

Jackson carefully placed the hammer on Dad's workbench, turned, and walked back across the alley. I wondered if he felt guilty for helping me instead of Aidan and Sawyer.

I sanded the inside of the crate. It needed to be smooth to keep splinters from digging into my behind. I got into the rhythm of the rough paper sliding across the wood, sounding like the beat of a snare drum keeping time to Les Brown and his orchestra. The *swish-swish-swish* drowned out the sounds of the occasional car crunching the gravel of Satan's Sidewalk. Sawdust stuck to the sweat on my forehead, and the smell of raw wood mixed with the stale scent of oil and dirt. I put all my muscle into it, concentrating on filing the splinters into dust. That's why Anne's voice surprised me.

"I knew it!"

I whirled around, sandpaper held in front of me like a shield, and Echo bolted from his napping spot. Anne stepped aside, letting him pass. "You couldn't stand the thought of being shown up by a girl, could you, Cory? You're just as bad as Sawyer."

"That's not true," I told her honestly. "But I am trying to make a better go-cart than *theirs*."

"Yeah?" she asked, studying my face as if she could see the truth written there. I couldn't help but notice the way her eyes got brighter when her smile wiped the scowl off her face. "Me, too! We should work together."

It stung a little, having her offer what my best friend wouldn't.

She walked around my supplies, feeling the wood and tapping her fingers on the crate. "This'll give whoever pushes you a firm base. It'll make it harder to fall off, too. How are you going to steer it?"

"A rope laced through two holes drilled in the front of the crate and tied at the ends of my two-by-four axle. I'm using your idea of attaching the front axle to the plywood base using a single eyebolt so the axle can pivot right or left with a tug of the rope."

Anne's eyes narrowed into slits. "You've been *spying* on me!"

"How else could we find out what you were up to?"

Anne glared at me a full ten seconds, then grinned again. "That's okay, because mine is still better than yours."

"Not a chance," I said.

"It is," she argued. "Mine could beat yours in a race because the crate will create wind drag."

"Is that a dare?" I asked with a voice full of bravado, but inside I worried she might be right about the crate slowing down my go-cart.

"I'm ready whenever you are," Anne said, but she said it like it was only a game instead of some kind of battle.

"Give me one more week."

"You're on! Until then, come and help me with mine."

I didn't want Sawyer and Aidan to sneak in and steal any of my ideas so I covered my cart with an old sheet. Then I closed up the garage and crossed Satan's Sidewalk to where Anne was pulling her cart across the yard. She tried to act like it was as normal as pulling a Radio Flyer, but I saw her swell with pride. I couldn't blame her. A go-cart was much better than a little red wagon. Echo rubbed against a wheel, then looked up at me as if to say he approved, too.

Anne sat down on the painted plywood and grabbed the rope, holding it like it was the reins to a horse. "Push me to the square so I can test the steering."

I leaned into Anne's shoulders, pushing her go-cart over the bumpy backyard and around the side of the house to the front sidewalk. Her shoulder blades were small and sharp compared to Sawyer or Aidan's, but there was nothing weak about her as she tugged the ropes. Echo followed us to the corner before fading back into the shadows.

The square's crisscrossing sidewalks made a perfect test track as long as people got off the sidewalk to let us pass. Anne had done a good job, but the wheels from her old baby carriage felt every bump and crack on the sidewalk. Her shoulders were bound to be bruised from where I pushed.

I was looking at how the sun made a perfect halo of shine on the top of her head, so I didn't see Aidan and Sawyer until they crossed Main Street and stepped right in our way. Anne's whole body leaned left as she steered to miss them. The cart jerked right, thumped off the edge of the sidewalk, and banged into the base of the statue. I glanced up at Grandpa as if he might be ready to yell at us, but he still wore the same unblinking stare.

Sawyer laughed, nearly choking on his gum. Aidan circled Anne's cart to get a good look.

"No way yours will be better than mine," Anne told them right off.

Sawyer glared at me. "You told her what we were doing?"

"Don't blame Cory," Anne said. "I could hear you through the walls of Aidan's garage. It's not like you were quiet or anything. I can spy just as well as you can. Even if I am a *girl*."

"She was going to f-f-find out anyway," Aidan pointed out to Sawyer.

Anne plopped her feet over the sides of the plywood. "You want a turn?"

"I thought you'd n-n-never ask," Aidan said and climbed on the cart.

Sawyer settled against the statue to watch how the go-cart handled while I helped Anne push Aidan around the statue. We started out slow, easing the cart toward the sidewalk that circled the park. The old wheels made a racket, but we didn't care. It didn't take long for Aidan to get the hang of tugging the ropes to make the front axle swivel.

"F-F-Faster!" Aidan hollered over his shoulder.

I leaned into his shoulder, pushing for all I was worth. Anne matched me step for step. Aidan was nearly bent double, but the go-cart picked up speed. We sprinted around the park, then cut back across the middle. The wheels rattled on the sidewalk as we urged the go-cart faster and faster. Aidan whooped as we hurtled past my grandfather. Sawyer was nothing but a blur.

Aidan muscled the ropes, struggling to steer around the base of the statue. I leaned into his shoulder to give him a boost. We were working together and it felt good. Just like old times.

And then Sawyer yelled, "Watch out!"

Aidan jerked the rope. The cart yawed to the right and bounced off the sidewalk, barely missing Mr. Ziegler and his two giant wolfhounds walking on the far side of the statue. Anne struggled to keep her balance, and I slipped off the sidewalk's edge and rolled to the ground.

The massive dogs growled, but Ziegler jerked the leashes, the black case he clutched banging against the base of the statue with his sudden movement. "Odin, Pandora. *Sitz!*" His throaty accent sent my stomach tumbling. The monsters sat on their haunches, but they didn't take their eyes off of us. Neither did Ziegler.

"We're sorry, Mr. Ziegler," Anne said. "We didn't see you."

"You muzt learn to vatch where you go," he said, his mouth pulled down in a crooked frown. "Zomeone could get hurt."

When I stood up, one of the dogs growled.

"*Bleib!*" Ziegler reminded the dogs in a calm voice. "*Braver Hund! Braver Hund!*"

The spit in my mouth evaporated and I froze, waiting for them to break that tiny rope and go for my throat. Anne must've thought the same thing.

"Your dogs really are big," she said. "Will those little ropes hold them?"

Ziegler inspected her over the tops of his glasses. "They vill ztay," he said, not really answering her question.

Then Anne asked what Aidan and I had wondered about ever since Ziegler moved to Satan's Sidewalk. "What keeps them from jumping your gate and running away?"

"They are trained," Mr. Ziegler said. "My dogz obey."

I glanced at Sawyer to make sure he was listening when I asked my own question. "Who trained them?"

Ziegler turned his gaze to me, and one corner of his mouth lifted in a half-smile. "I did, of course," he said. "But my dogz, they do not like to be teased. You vould be wise to remember zat. All of you."

He looked directly at the place where my cap should've been before turning his attention back to his dogs. "Odin, Pandora," he said in a voice as serious as death. The dogs' ears twitched as their massive heads swiveled to face him. "*Fuß!*"

The monsters found their places by Mr. Ziegler, one on each side. Pandora smacked her lips and gave us a final look before following Mr. Ziegler past my grandfather's statue.

The Warrior Kid would have zapped Ziegler and his hounds with death rays right then and there, but since I didn't have any superpowers, all I could do was watch him go. "Did you hear that? He admitted it. He trained those dogs and he'll sic them on anyone who gets in his way."

Sawyer gave me a little shove between my shoulder blades. "Then this is your chance, Cory. Put your money where your mouth is and stop your Nazi spy. Or are you just going to let him walk away?"

"You're both knuckleheads," Anne told him. "There's nothing sinister about Ziegler."

"He's G-G-German," Aidan reminded Anne. "That makes him g-g-guilty by association."

"Not all Germans are bad," she said.

"They are in my book," I told her.

"You're wrong, Cory. Saying all Germans are bad is the same as saying a girl can't knock a baseball across the square or pound a nail in a plank of plywood. And we all know that's not true."

Anne stood on one side of her go-cart. We stood on the other. She crossed her arms, put one foot on her cart, and stared us down in victory.

Sawyer shifted his wad of gum and spat at the wheel of her go-cart. "You're full of beans. Come on, Aidan. Let's go build a real go-cart that puts this one to shame."

As I watched Aidan and Sawyer march through the shadows of my grandfather's statue, I tried to ignore the bubble of doubt boiling up until it popped as one giant question.

What if Anne was right about Ziegler?

14

THE COLOR OF DEATH

O n Friday, Mom fixed me a peanut butter sandwich for lunch. It was too hot for anything else. I had the latest Space Warrior comic book on the table by my plate. Before Dad left, I wasn't allowed to read at the table, but Mom didn't say anything about it now. After all, she had Dad's letters filed in a basket on the table right next to the salt and pepper shakers.

I pulled the crusts off my bread while reading about the Warrior locked in another battle with his nemesis. I liked how the Warrior stood with his arms on his hips, facing his archenemy without a flinch of fear. He even smiled as flames bounced off his helmet. Laughing in the face of evil. That's what a hero does.

Echo wrapped around my ankles and I reached down to run my hand along his back.

"Don't pet the cat while you're eating," Mom said without looking up from the letter Dad had written last month.

119

Echo weaved through the chair legs and paused at Mom's ankles. I grinned when she reached down to rub the space between his ears without even thinking.

The radio static was almost in time to Benny Goodman's "Taking a Chance on Love," and a fly buzz-thumped against the blackout curtain pulled back from the kitchen window. Everything was normal and dull and boring, so the knock on the front door seemed unnaturally loud.

Mom looked at me. I looked at her, the letter from Dad floating from her fingers down to the table in a lazy zigzag.

The sound of our chairs scratching the floor as we scooted back spooked Echo and he took off running. I followed Mom out of the kitchen. Through the dining room. Into the living room. Past the big double window that Mom casually glanced out.

She stopped, then, so fast that I almost stepped on her heel. Her breath caught in her throat like a hiccup and one hand moved toward her face only to stop and hang in midair as if she forgot it was attached to her arm. "Oh," she whispered. She took three quick breaths without letting any of them out before saying it again. "Oh."

I looked out the window to see what had caught her attention.

They had come when we weren't watching. When our guard was down. In a shiny Army car with the official C gas ration sticker proudly displayed in the window.

"They must be lost," I said. It was the only thing that

made sense. "They have the wrong address. It's a mistake. I'll tell them, Mom. I'll let them know."

Another knock on the door caused Mom to shudder and the hand that had been hanging in the air found my arm to stop me. "No," she said. "I'll get it. It has to be me."

I watched her walk to the door and pause, staring at it as if she'd forgotten how to work the doorknob, until another knock rattled it. Then her head gave a little jerk and she took a breath before opening the door to face two men standing there.

"Mrs. Woodford?" asked the man wearing a dress uniform. I recognized him from a fuzzy photograph Dad had sent us from boot camp, but I couldn't remember his name. The man didn't seem to need an answer, since he took Mom by the elbow and gently led her right back the way she had just walked—all the way back into the living room to the sofa. His actions were full of practice and memory.

"I'm sorry, Mrs. Woodford," the officer said in a quiet, even voice as he gently placed a silver chain in Mom's hand and then curled her fingers around it. He pulled a Western Union telegram from his pocket, staring at the words, waiting as if he thought they might change. Finally he started to read. "It's my duty to inform you that there was an accident in France a little over a week ago."

Mom's fingers played over the chain as if it were a Catholic rosary. Dog tags, they were called. One to leave on a fallen soldier. One to notify the family. Name. Rank.

Serial number. Religion. The identification that soldiers wore until they didn't need it anymore. There was only one tag on the chain sliding through Mom's fingers.

"I knew your husband in boot camp. He told me about his father. And Cory and you. I didn't want you to hear this from a telegram, Mrs. Woodford." The officer laid the paper on the sofa next to Mom and patted it as if he could settle the words into the cushion. He kept talking. I tried to listen, but his words didn't quite go together and they ended up as phrases getting lost somewhere between his mouth and my ears.

"It was an explosion in the camp. A spark ignited by something your husband triggered."

"It was a mistake. A horrible mistake," said the other man, the one wearing the white collar.

I shook my head. That just wasn't right. It couldn't be. "No. No. NO!" I interrupted. "*You're* the ones making a mistake. My dad is a Woodford. A hero. He's saving the world. Dad would never do something stupid like that! Take it back. Take. It. BACK!"

The priest walked across the room and put his arm around my shoulder. "I'm so sorry," he said. "This is a terrible thing, to lose your father. We must pray for his soul."

"He's in France," the officer went on to tell Mom. "Your husband was buried in France."

Buried. My father was *buried*. And that's when the

words became real and I knew that it was too late. Too late to pray. Too late for my dad.

The men talked to Mom about benefits and where we could get help while I stood there, stuck in that nowhere land between the front door and the living room. I stared at the hole in the rug where Dad had dropped a bit of ash last Christmas, and twisted my comic book tighter and tighter until I felt the cover tear. Even then I didn't stop.

It surprised me the way Mom sat so straight. Rigid, like my grandfather's statue. Totally still except for the way her throat jerked with tiny twitches every time she swallowed. Her eyes looked hard and shiny at the officer, but she didn't say anything. Not a single word.

It didn't make sense. Why didn't she scream that they were wrong? They had to be. Heroes don't die from making a *mistake*.

"If there's anything we can do, let us know," the priest finally said, leaving my side so he could reach down and help Mom stand. Her hands were still rubbing the chain of Dad's dog tag, so he had to take her arms instead. He didn't let go of her until they moved past me to the front door, where he paused long enough to mutter a prayer. The words were garbled and blurred together like a song from a different country. Then he nodded to Mom and stepped through the door.

The officer looked me in the eyes before following the priest. "You're the man of the house, now," he said.

He reached out, planning to squeeze my shoulder, but I stepped back from his touch. He raised his hand to his forehead in a silent salute instead.

He turned then, and they both walked down our sidewalk. I watched them get in that shiny car with the C gas ration sticker. Heard the click of the key. The engine turned and the wheels shushed down the street, sounding like the Mallory ghosts whispering acid-laden lies.

I saw curtains twitch in the house across the street, and one of Ziegler's hounds barked down at the bottom of the alley. Echo paused in the hallway, one paw frozen in the air as if he planned to claw through silence thick enough to smother us.

Mom didn't move. Not at first. Except for another twitchy swallow that ended in a choked gasp.

"Mom?" I whispered. "Mom?"

My voice jolted her back from the door and she stumbled, as if the earth had heaved up right beneath her feet. She hit the wall hard, scaring Echo so bad he left claw marks in the hardwood floor as he fled back to the kitchen.

"He said he'd come back," Mom said, her stony look finally crumbling as she slid down the wall. I reached out, but I still had my comic book in my hands and I couldn't catch her before she landed on the floor in a ball. She held her head, the silver of Dad's chain resting on her hair like a crown. "He promised," she said, her voice breaking with a sob. "He *promised*."

I'd never heard Mom cry before, and my own eyes stung

as I choked on a vile taste in the back of my throat. I didn't know what to do, so I stood there and stared at my comic book for answers.

The Kid had to be steady.

Rock solid.

Woodford Brave.

"Heroes. Don't. Cry," I whispered. "Heroes. Don't. Cry."

Mom reached up, the dog tag dangling from her fingers. She snatched the comic book from my hands and hurled it through the open door. "To hell they don't!" she screamed, her voice raw enough to bleed. Then she grabbed my wrist, pulling me down to the floor so she could wrap her arms around me, burying my face against her shoulder.

I tried to be strong. To be the man I was supposed to be. I tried to be like Grandpa. Like Dad. But there were too many tears to hold back. So we sat on the floor, Mom and me, rocking back and forth. Clinging to each other while our world fell apart.

And that is how the blue star in our window changed to gold.

Blue for the living. Gold for the dead.

15

WOODFORD BRAVE

The neighbors came after that, bringing cakes and ham and biscuits as if feeding us could fill up the giant hole where my dad should've been. Mrs. Springgate seemed to camp out in the kitchen, switching out platters of sandwiches and cookies.

Aidan came with his mom and dad. Jackson, too. Mr. Franklin and his wife brought a basket of jams. I almost didn't recognize Mrs. Baird without the big straw hat covered in flowers. Mom always seemed to find me. To be there with her hand on my shoulder or squeezing me to her side in a hug. And I tried to do the same for her. Sometimes it was hard to know who was holding the other one up. I guess it didn't really matter as long as we stayed standing.

Even Sawyer came. His mother had two loaves of homemade bread. Sawyer handed me a new Space Warrior comic book. "I'm sorry, Cory," he said. "Really sorry. I never meant all those things I said about the Woodfords. I know your dad was brave."

I didn't know how to answer. What good were words, anyway?

Every time Mom answered the door, it was a battle. A fight to keep standing. Keep smiling. Be polite. She was a different kind of Woodford Brave. When she opened the door to Ziegler, I thought she'd spit in his eye and slam the door on his fingers. But instead she actually invited him in for coffee and cake.

I couldn't believe Ziegler had the nerve to walk in our house. Not after what fighting the Nazis had cost us. But there he was. Tall. Skinny. Pushing his glasses up on his nose.

Even worse: he twisted my cap in his hand. The last thing Dad had ever given to me. I guess his dogs hadn't chewed it up after all, though it was dirty and the bill was bent. The sight of him holding it burned a hole in my stomach, and if it hadn't been for Mrs. Springgate standing there, I might've barreled into the living room and tackled him to the ground. Instead, I reached out and took my cap when he handed it to me, mumbling a *thank you* because I knew that was what Mom expected me to say. It felt good to have my cap back, even though it had been in the hands of a German. I tried to imagine feeling something left over from my dad woven in the fabric, a surge of power or a bolt of energy. Something, anything, from Dad.

At night I'd lie in bed, staring at the dark. Echo liked to sleep curled up near my pillow. He'd wake now and then to reach out a paw, resting it on my cheek or chin. Sometimes I thought I could hear the Mallory ghosts moaning at the bottom of Satan's Sidewalk. I wondered if they were doomed to spend eternity fighting over whether Cyn should dance or not. At least they could still talk to each other.

Mrs. Springgate was always around, even when I got out of bed in the mornings. As far as I could remember she had never been in our house, but she acted as if she knew every nook and cranny. She made breakfast, dusted the living room, cleaned the bathroom. Sometimes I heard her talking with Mom in a low voice. I wondered if she gave Mom some of her beer. I thought about telling Dad, but then it hit me. I couldn't. I would never be able tell Dad anything again.

For a week, I stayed in my room. I read my comic books. Then read them again, paying attention to what the Warrior did whenever someone died. How did he look? What did he say?

The Warrior never cried. He went after the bad guys. He sought revenge.

I stood in front of my mirror and practiced being the Kid. Face blank. Eyes cold. Fists clenched. My sidekick, the Mighty Echo, at my side. Both of us silent. Stoic.

Woodford Brave.

I left the window wide open at night, not even bothering with the blackout curtains, and listened for the ghosts to call out. The whole idea of ghosts started making sense. What else happened to a person's feelings and thoughts, all their knowledge and energy, all the words and laughter that had made them who they were? That couldn't just be gone in a split second. It had to float around, looking for a place to land. It made sense that all the energy that made up a person would seek a familiar place. Someplace they had lived and worked and played. Where they had people who wanted to see them just one more time.

After a week my room started feeling too small, and I fled the house filled with people saying words that wouldn't change a thing. How could they know how I felt or what I thought? What made them think they could tell me how to behave or what my father would want?

My go-cart sat in the middle of the garage. Dad's tools were scattered on the workbench, and the pile of rags Echo used for naps was still a tangled heap in the corner. Dust motes swirled and shifted in a sunbeam, hinting at a solid shape, only to churn apart as if something walked through them. I turned in a circle. Dad had died thousands of miles away, in a land where they didn't even speak our language. If there were such things as ghosts, would he wander in a foreign land, lost for all eternity? Or would he, could he, find his way here, where he had spent hours polishing the tools he never really used? Where he could watch over me?

"I won't let you down, Dad," I whispered to the dust motes. "I promise."

I searched the sunbeam, but the dust stayed dust, so

I grabbed the hammer and started working on my go-cart. I worked on it all day, and I went back to the garage every day after that. After a few days, Anne showed up. She didn't say anything. Not one single word. Just picked up a piece of sandpaper and started smoothing away the wood on the crate. We worked like that, in quiet. I focused on the wood and sandpaper and nails. And sometimes on Anne's breath, on the way she moved and the way her blue eyes darted to mine and stayed there, unafraid, but not expecting anything. Just there.

I wondered where Aidan was, but when I heard Sawyer hooting from across Satan's Sidewalk one afternoon, I knew. It wasn't fair that their lives went on just like always when my entire world had been destroyed. Not fair that they still had their dads. Even if Aidan's father had a bum leg and Sawyer's would rather sit in a tavern instead of fighting the Nazi aggression. It. Wasn't. Fair.

I focused on the wood of the crate that was supposed to be my tank. If only Dad had had a tank to protect him from flying debris. Or the Kid's Net of Invincibility. Even if he'd just had on his own helmet. But he hadn't, and a ragged shard from an exploding jeep had pierced his brain. He may not have been fighting in battle, but I knew one thing. If it hadn't been for the Germans wanting to take over the world, my dad would've still been safe right here in Harmony, helping me build go-carts and make slingshots. Telling me what to do about Aidan and Sawyer. And Ziegler.

"I'm sorry about your dad, Cory."

Anne stood up from tightening a screw and faced the open door, but I didn't need to turn around to know it was Jackson leaning against the garage.

"What good is sorry?"

"You're right, Cory. Sorry doesn't do one bit of good, does it?"

I held Dad's hammer. My hand looked small, skinny. Dad's had been big with calluses on the palms. I doubted my hand would ever grow as strong as his.

Jackson turned to leave, but I stopped him. "There is something you can do."

He half-turned, waiting.

"When you get over there, kill every last German you see. Do it for Dad."

Jackson used his thumbnail to flick a chip of paint from the garage doorframe. "Whatever you say, Cory. Whatever you say."

Anne watched him walk away, then met my eyes, finally breaking her silence. "Having a parent die is hard. I know."

Anne had only mentioned her mother once. I'd pretty much forgotten that she was even dead.

"Everyone says things get better with time," she said. "But the hurt doesn't ever go away. Not really. You'll always miss your dad, Cory. Sort of like when you lose a tooth and you keep poking your tongue where it used to be, feeling the hole even though that makes it hurt more. But after a while, you get used to the feel of it and you don't look for the hole as much."

"I'll never get used to it," I whispered.

"You still get hungry, don't you? You still sneeze? Your nose still runs, right? So you eat and sneeze and blow your nose. One thing follows another. Life goes on, Cory. Just by putting one foot in front of the other you'll get to the other side of grief. But hating people who had nothing to do with what happened to your dad won't help."

I turned on her then, so fast that she took a step back. "How can you say that? If it hadn't been for the Germans, my dad would be right here, helping me build this go-cart instead of you."

"Not all Germans are bad," she said. "You have to know that."

Anne seemed so sure. As if the words she spoke were written on Moses's tablet when he came off the mountain. But then I looked at Dad's hammer in my hand. My hammer now. "You don't know anything, Anne, but I do. You're nothing but a dumb Dora. Ziegler's one of the bad guys and it's up to me to do something about it."

Then I pounded a nail so hard the wood splintered in two.

16

THE REVENGE OF THE WARRIOR KID AND THE MIGHTY ECHO

~~Dear Dad~~

All the white space of the paper stared up at me. I started to draw, hoping it would help me block out the sound of Mom crying.

THE KID KNELT BY THE WARRIOR'S LIFELESS BODY. "YOU WILL BE AVENGED!" HE ROARED, PUMPING HIS FISTS IN THE AIR. THEN HE STOOD AND FACED HIS ARCHENEMY.

"BWA-HA-HA," LAUGHED THE EVIL SPY. "YOU CANNOT STOP ME NOW!"
THE SPY AND HIS ARMY OF GHOSTS WITH
SWASTIKAS WHERE THEIR EYES SHOULD BE SPREAD
OVER THE LANDSCAPE LIKE BLACK OIL SPILLING
DOWN SATAN'S SIDEWALK.

THE KID TOOK A STEP, AND HIS HYPERSPEED BOOTS CLANGED AGAINST SOMETHING
BURIED IN THE RUBBLE. THE HELMET OF POWER! HE FLICKED AWAY THE DIRT
AND PLACED IT ON HIS HEAD, BUT HE FAILED TO FEEL THE SURGE OF POWER.

HAD THE WARRIOR'S POWER DIED WITH HIM?

THE LEGION OF GHOSTLY SOLDIERS WERE UPON THE KID. HE COULD NOT RUN. THE KID NEVER RAN. AT LEAST HE WAS NOT ALONE. HIS SIDEKICK STOOD BRAVELY AT HIS SIDE.

THE MIGHTY ECHO LASHED OUT WITH HIS DAGGER CLAWS,
LEAVING TRAILS OF VILE GREEN ACID BLOOD SPILLING FROM THE GHOSTS' ROTTING FLESH.

THE ENEMY SPY SURVEYED THE CARNAGE. HIS LAUGHTER ECHOED OVER THE LANDSCAPE, WHICH HAD BEEN CRATERED BY A BLITZKRIEG OF ACID BOMBS. THE NEARBY HUMAN ENCAMPMENT HAD BEEN CRUSHED AND THE RUBBLE OF A JEEP SURROUNDED THE KID. ITS PIECES SPREAD FAR AND WIDE BY AN EXPLOSION IMPOSSIBLE TO SURVIVE.

A BEAUTIFUL QUEEN CRADLED THE DEAD WARRIOR, HER TEARS FLOWING TO THE GROUND.

I ignored the wet splotches that smeared the face of the Kid. After all, the Kid never cried.

"We'll get them," I told Echo. "Every. Last. One."

17

PERFECT PLAN

"What if he s-s-sees us?" Aidan asked.

It was Friday night and the sun was low in the sky. It hadn't taken long to convince Sawyer of my plan. All I had to do was tell him I was ready to prove, once and for all, that I was a Woodford through and through. Since Sawyer was in, so was Aidan. That, and they were both being extra nice since Dad died. Now all of us were huddled in Aidan's living room, trying to see through a crack in the curtains. Even Anne.

"Ziegler's as regular as clockwork," I repeated for the umpteenth time. "We won't even need the Space Warrior's x-ray goggles to follow him."

Sawyer grinned. "Maybe I was wrong about you, Cory. You're really stepping up to the plate this time."

I wasn't sure if he meant it or if he was just being nice. "I told you I'd prove he's a spy, and I meant it."

"You're full of beans," Anne said. "Ziegler's no more a spy than I am."

"Said the girl p-p-peeking out a window," Aidan pointed out.

"You don't have to go," I added. "Nobody's making you."

"I'm your friend, Cory," she said. "Of course I'll go."

Sawyer made kissy noises on his arm. "Sounds like Cory's girlfriend can't live without him."

"Cory and Anne, s-s-sitting in a tree, k-i-s-s-i-n-g," chanted Aidan.

"Shut up," I said, hoping the light was dim enough that none of them could see my ears burning.

Anne acted like Aidan hadn't said a thing. "Even if he is a spy, Cory, catching him won't bring back your dad."

"The Germans killed my father. They have to pay for what they did."

"No matter how many times you say it," Anne said softly, "it doesn't make it true."

"I'm avenging his death. It's what superheroes do."

Anne didn't have an answer to that.

"Shh," Aidan said. "He's c-c-coming."

Ziegler's shadow, long and skinny, led the way as he strode up the block. The same black case he always carried dangled from his right arm. He kept his eyes forward without so much as a glance our way.

"This is it," I said, adjusting my cap low over my eyes and heading for the door. It felt good having my cap back, even it if had been in the hands of the enemy.

"Let's go c-c-catch a spy," Aidan said.

It happened just like I planned. As soon as Ziegler passed Aidan's house, we flew out the back door. I became the Kid, leading my friends up Satan's Sidewalk to where it dumped onto a street. I held out my hand, stopping them until I saw Ziegler crossing at the corner. Then I darted to where the alley continued on the other side of the street. Up three blocks, then zigzagging to another. We tracked Ziegler for fifteen minutes until he slowed and crossed one final street, heading for the last place I expected him to go.

The VFW.

The VFW was tucked on the side of town one block north of the grain elevator. Dinners, reunions, and dances all happened at the VFW. Food and booze was cheap for soldiers, and a band played most nights. Dad took Mom dancing there the last time he was home on leave. The very last time.

"That really came out of left field," Sawyer said, as Ziegler pulled open the door and waited for a group of men dressed in Navy whites to file in.

"It makes perfect sense," I said slowly, thinking it through out loud. "The VFW is the best place in Harmony for a Nazi spy to collect information on the sly. When soldiers come home on leave, they hang out at the VFW. They drink a few beers and that gets them talking. It's a spot-on plan to overhear secrets."

"Or maybe he just wants to boogie-woogie," Anne said.

"There's one way to find out," I told her.

"Forget it," Anne said before I could take a step toward the VFW. "No kids allowed."

A cluster of girls wearing high heels went inside. One of them had tried to draw a line down the back of her leg to make it look like she was wearing stockings, but the line was crooked. When they pulled open the door, the sound of laughter reached out to us.

I was the Kid. Nothing would stop me from completing my mission.

"Follow me."

I led them around back to the alley littered with crates, wood, and trash. I pointed to the three small windows high on the outside wall. They were propped open to encourage what little breeze there was to cool off the dancers inside. Cigarette smoke mingling with stale beer stained the air.

"They're too high for us to see inside," Anne said.

"Not a problem." I started pulling crates toward the back of the building. Aidan caught on, then Sawyer. Soon we had enough to build a pyramid under the window. If we squeezed real close, we could all stand on the top, but we had to be careful not to tip over. I pushed my cap back on my head so it wouldn't bump the grimy window, then curled my fingers around the sill to peek inside.

The VFW was dimly lit. Tables lined the edges of the room. My heart double-thumped at the sight of two men wearing Army green. One of them looked just like Dad. I gripped the window ledge and blinked hard to clear my vision. The Kid didn't cry. My eyes were just blurry from the smoke curling through the window.

The floor had seen better days. Dark marks and scratches from years of dancing crisscrossed the grain of the wood. There were a few groups of men and more clusters of women. The women were laughing, trying not to look as if they were eyeballing the men. Right beneath us was a platform stage that stood two feet higher than the dance floor.

Ziegler walked through the doors at the front of the room, looking straight ahead as if there wasn't another soul in the room.

"He doesn't look like he's trying to extract military secrets and invasion plans from anyone," Anne pointed out.

"Give him time," I said.

The cuffs of Ziegler's baggy pants broke on wing-tipped shoes that matched the shine of his black hair. The fingers of his right hand curled around the handle of his beat-up black case. He walked clear across the floor and swung it gently so that it didn't make a sound when it landed on the stage. There were latches on the case, and he flicked them open with his little finger.

A trio of girls came in wearing cherry rouge and platform shoes. Navy boys wearing caps cocked to one side whistled through their teeth.

"We ought to w-w-warn them," Aidan said, but none of us cried out.

Ziegler never looked up. It was as if he was alone. Just him and that case. He tossed back the lid and took out a muddy pink cloth. Then he lifted what was inside.

It wasn't secret documents. Not guns or knives or bombs, either.

The single light in the middle of the room sent a shiny beacon slicing through the smoke-fog of the club to land on a trumpet.

Ziegler looked deep into the trumpet's brass and I imagined his brown eyes staring back as if from a mirror. He ran the cloth over the smooth gleam of the horn's long, thin lines and swelling curves. He polished his trumpet until all the tables were filled with people. Finally, he dropped the cloth back in his case and hopped onto the stage, quick and lithe like Echo jumping from the floor to a windowsill. A few other band members stepped up, too, but they soon faded behind him as he tested the give of the brass valves. Then he placed the horn to his lips and the music began.

Ziegler worked the crowd, starting soft and sad, sliding from one note to another with lazy self-assurance. The band followed his music as it led the dancers in a two-step. Soft curls rested on women's necks as they smiled up at partners, their Victory-red lips laughed, and they stepped in time.

Not a single one seemed to care that a German was in their midst.

One song ended and another began. Ziegler's back arched and he blew his trumpet loud and jazzy, letting the notes tumble and swell. His slicked-back hair worked loose and his white shirt stuck to his back. The glitter ball twirled above, throwing sparkles like big drops of sweat on the dancers, on the band, and on him.

Smoke hovered overhead as his parade of notes carried the dancers across the scarred wooden floor. I squinted through the swirling haze to catch a glimpse of his fingers flying on valves in a mysterious code of quarter-notes and swing time. My toes, my fingers, the beat of my heart, all pounded to the rhythm of his trumpet. He was better than Les Brown. Even better than Tommy Dorsey.

I stared at Ziegler, swaying and twisting as he blew that horn until suddenly he was looking right at me. He didn't blink. Didn't miss a beat before he turned back to face the dancers again.

I jumped down, swiping the cap off my head, even though it was too late. The Kid's cover was already blown. The Space Warrior would've been humiliated.

Anne hopped down beside me. She was laughing so hard she snorted. Then she said the four words every kid hates—coming from Anne, they were even worse. "I told you so!"

"She's just whiffing at hot air," Sawyer said, shattering any doubts that I might have had into a thousand jagged slivers. "Your girlfriend's nothing but a dumb Dora."

"She is *not* my girlfriend," I said. "She's not even a friend. No friend of mine would side with a German. Not after what they did to my father."

I looked Anne in the eyes. "Ziegler's one of *them*. He's a bad guy. He's to blame for what happened to Dad."

"Face it, Cory. You weren't fair to Mr. Ziegler. You should've gotten to know the man he *is* instead of plunking him in a category based on where he happened to be born. I know it, and you know it, too. You just won't admit it."

Sawyer stood on one side of me, Aidan on the other. We were a formidable force. I willed Anne's words to bounce off me and said the words the Warrior said each and every time he faced down his archenemy. "*Nothing* is fair when it comes to evil."

Anne stepped back as if she'd been slapped, but she didn't blink. Then she turned and walked away. I reached up, adjusted my ball cap, and watched her go.

18

HERO'S ACT OR COWARD'S SCARE?

The moon was a jack-o'-lantern grin in the sky as we zigzagged back through the alleys of Harmony. The memory of Ziegler's trumpet followed, the notes vaguely familiar. Then it hit me. It was the same sound as the Mallory ghosts I heard at night. Now I knew it had been the faint music of Ziegler's trumpet the whole time.

"See you tomorrow, Cory," Sawyer said when we split up at Meeker Street. "You too, Aidan." He didn't say anything to Anne.

The houses we passed were dark and the alleys deserted as we made our way back to Satan's Sidewalk. The muffled war reports from radios leaking through blackout curtains blurred with the calls of cicadas. It was a shock to see one of the houses backing up to Satan's Sidewalk lit up like high noon.

"Oh, no," Anne said. "They've probably been looking all over for us."

I sprinted down the alley to the back of our houses. Mom had barely been holding it together. If she thought I was missing, she'd break into a million tiny pieces.

But the only movement at my house was Echo, emerging from shadows to rub against my legs as if he had been waiting the entire time just for me.

It was the back door to Aidan's house that stood wide open. Not a single blackout curtain had been pulled over the windows. Enough light cut slices out of the night to lead a hundred Nazi warplanes to our neighborhood. If the light didn't, the shouting would.

Aidan's dad was loud and full of growl. His mother's voice was so high-pitched I couldn't make out the words. Finally there was Jackson.

"I'm not going," Jackson yelled over the other voices. "I'm not fighting in any war. Ever!"

If Jackson had grown wings and announced he was the tooth fairy, I couldn't have been more surprised.

Aidan stopped, as if Jackson's words had enough power to freeze his hand to the gate.

His father's voice carried a note of pleading: "Think of Aidan. He looks up to you."

Jackson's voice shot back: "Don't bring Aidan into this. He's nothing but a little kid."

"Then think of us. You'll bring shame to us. To our family."

"You want me to murder other men just so you won't be embarrassed?"

146

His father's voice backed down a notch. "It's your patriotic duty, not murder."

Jackson appeared at the back door, a black shadow against the yellow light of the kitchen. "I'm no soldier and you know it. You've known it all my life." He turned his back to the kitchen and carried a suitcase down the three steps. He paused when he saw us standing at the gate.

"Wh-Wh-Where are you going?" Aidan whispered.

Jackson's eyes flitted to me, then back to Aidan. "Oregon."

"But you're l-l-leaving for Europe next month," Aidan said. "To f-f-fight the Nazis."

"Not me, little brother. Not me."

"You can't, J-J-Jackson. You can't. Everyone will think you're a *coward*." Aidan's voice dropped when he said the last word, as if the feel of it burned his tongue.

Jackson took a step toward Aidan. One arm was raised as if he planned to hug his little brother, but Aidan backed away. "Try not to hate me, okay?" Jackson said, letting his arm drop to his side. "Just try not to hate me too much."

He started walking down the alley, straight toward the Demons' Door. He had only taken three steps when he stopped once more, as if suddenly remembering something. This time he faced me. "I'm sorry, Cory," he said. "I'm sorry I'm not made of the same stuff as your comic book heroes. But you know what? I don't think your dad was, either. Nobody, and I mean nobody, is like that. In real life, everyone is scared witless. Bravery is just the disguise they wear to cover up the fear."

Then he turned and disappeared into the shadows. A sudden eruption of barks from Odin and Pandora announced when he reached the bottom of the alley.

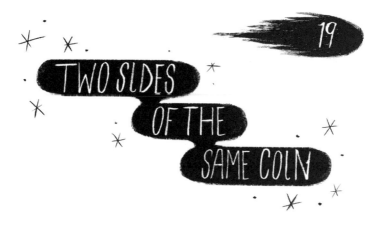

19

TWO SIDES OF THE SAME COIN

A heavy thud woke me the next morning.

"Mom? Mom? Are you okay?"

No answer.

I rushed to my parents' room. Mom's room now. She sat on the bed, a box on the floor at her feet. Her eyes were red and puffy. The covers were a jumbled heap, but only on one side. The other side was smooth without a single wrinkle.

"He didn't have much," Mom said, knowing I was there without even looking. "This is all that's left of him. A few shirts. Some shoes. How does a man live in a house his entire life and not leave anything of value behind except for a cardboard box of odds and ends and one silver coin?"

She turned Dad's lucky silver dollar in her fingers, creating a small pinprick of brightness in the room. From where I stood, I couldn't tell which side was heads and which was tails.

"Whenever he needed to make a decision he would reach in his pocket and rub this dollar as if he could rub out an answer," Mom said, her own fingers smoothing its surface. "I think he rubbed the face off Lady Liberty before finally enlisting."

That didn't make sense at all. "Dad wouldn't think twice about joining the Army. He was a Woodford. He knew what he had to do."

"Oh, Cory," Mom said, her words tangled in a sigh. She looked at me, drawing me into her tear-puddled eyes. "Your father didn't *want* to fight. He didn't want to leave you. Or me. But he felt that he *had* to."

I nodded, finally sure of what we were talking about. "Because he wasn't a coward like Jackson."

Mom stopped rubbing the coin. "What about Jackson?" she whispered.

I told her what had happened the night before, leaving out the part about spying on Ziegler. I waited for her to realize that I had sneaked out at night, but if she did, she didn't let on. "He said he was going west. To Oregon," I finished.

"That's where the conscientious objectors go," she said softly. "To a camp where they work for the government instead of fighting."

"Conscientious objectors?" I repeated. The words were hard to say, getting caught in my throat like a German curse word.

"Men who don't believe in fighting," she explained.

"Cowards, you mean?"

Mom's eyes changed in that instant, as if they had

turned to frozen pond water. "It takes a brave man to stand up for his beliefs. To turn his back on everything his friends and family say. To speak a truth that's different than everyone else's. It's a different kind of courage, Cory, but courage just the same. I just wish to God your father had been *that* kind of brave. At least he'd still be alive."

"But he would've ruined the Woodford name," I said, my words webbed in whisper as I tried to make sense of what she had said.

"What good is a reputation to a dead man?"

She absently turned the silver dollar over and over in the palm of her hand, but then she stopped to look at it as if it was the first time she'd ever seen it. Reaching out, she grabbed my wrist and pulled me toward her so she could lay it in my palm. Then she curled my fingers around it. "Take this, Cory. Use it to make good decisions. Just remember that there are always two sides to everything."

My eyes smarted at the feel of the cool metal, the smoothness of the silver. I wrapped my fingers around it, making it the center of my fist. "I hate the Germans. I hate them for starting this war. I hate them for what they did to Dad."

The color of Mom's face drained, but her eyes never left mine, reminding me of how Anne had peered at me last night in the alley behind the VFW. "Understand this," Mom said. "War isn't about the people from a faraway country. It's not about where a person is born and raised. It's about money and land and power."

"Exactly," I said. "The Germans want it all. They started this war and I hate them for it. Every. Single. One."

Mom pulled me close and wrapped her arms around me, resting her chin on my head. "Do you hate me, Cory?"

She was speaking English, but her words were gibberish. I stepped back so I could look at her. "Of course I don't hate you."

"But my great-grandmother's real last name was Kuhljuergen. Before she changed it to Collier."

The German name hit me in the gut like a cannonball and I stumbled until my back was against the wall. "No," I whispered. "No."

Mom ran her fingers over the delicate blue lines just beneath the surface of the skin on one of her wrists. "That blood you hate so much runs through these veins. Yours, too."

"But . . . but everyone hates the Germans."

"Be careful, Cory. Hatred is very dangerous," she said. "It's the worst weapon in this big ugly world."

I stood there with my back against the wall, watching my mother turn away from me and place a pair of mismatched socks in the box that was all we had left of my father.

THE UNDERCOVER ADVENTURES OF THE KID AND HIS MIGHTY ECHO

20

I laid the silver dollar on top of my desk and stared at the stack of blank paper next to it. I had believed Ziegler was a spy. Franklin, too. Just because they were German. And all summer I'd worked to convince Aidan and Sawyer. "What if they find out I'm German, too?" I whispered.

Echo's ears swiveled toward me, and he batted at the pencil. "Mrr-oww." I barely caught the pencil before it rolled off the edge of the desk.

"No one can know the truth," I told the Mighty Echo, punctuating each word with a sharp, straight line on the paper. "No. One. Can. Ever. Know."

THE KID HAD SEARCHED DEEP WITHIN HIS SOUL FOR A SPARK OF THE WARRIOR'S POWER. BUT HE FOUND NOTHING.

WHAM!

NOW HIS HYPERSPEED BOOTS TEETERED OVER THE EDGE OF A CLIFF WHILE THE MIGHTY ECHO CROUCHED BESIDE HIM.

TOGETHER, THEY FOUGHT VALIANTLY TO SHIELD THE QUEEN FROM CERTAIN DEATH. HER PULSING BLOOD SWELLED THE VEINS OF HER WRISTS, THROBBING AND POUNDING AS IT TRIED TO BURST FREE. SHE HELD A SECRET SO IMMENSE THAT REPEATING IT WOULD SHATTER THE VERY CORE OF THE PLANET ON WHICH THEY STOOD.

ONLY THE KID KNEW THE TRUTH, AND HE COULD NOT—WOULD NOT—BETRAY HER TRUST. NOT NOW. NOT EVER. HE HAD MADE A PROMISE TO THE WARRIOR. AND EVEN THOUGH THE WARRIOR HAD PERISHED, HE WOULD PROTECT THE QUEEN. NO. MATTER. WHAT. THE X OF IMPENETRABLE GLUE HE'D SEALED OVER HIS LIPS WAS PROOF THAT HE WOULD CARRY THE SECRET TO HIS GRAVE.

THE FORCE FIELD FROM THE HELMET OF POWER FAILED, ITS POWER BLEEDING INTO THE GROUND AND MIXING WITH THE TEARS OF THE QUEEN.

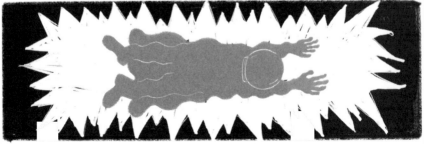

THE MANIACAL SPY AND HIS ZOMBIE SOLDIERS BLITZKRIEGED HIM AGAIN AND AGAIN.

A TRIO OF GHOSTS DROPPED ACID BOMBS, CRACKING THE GROUND INTO A JIGSAW PUZZLE OF DOOM.

IN THE DISTANCE, TWO NEW GHOSTS SWIRLED IN AGONY, SCREAMING OUT FOR REVENGE ON THEIR UNJUST DEATHS. AT THE BOTTOM OF THE ABYSS STOOD A NEW FOE. A FOE BORN OF LIES AND BETRAYAL. SHE AIMED A SLINGSHOT LOADED WITH MOLTEN LAVA, HER PIERCING BLUE EYES GLARING AT HIM FROM A CONSTELLATION OF FRECKLES SPLATTERED ACROSS HER CHEEKS.

TWO BOYS LOBBED STONES AT HER, DARING HER TO KNOCK THE KID FROM THE CLIFF.

THEY WERE ALL AGAINST HIM: EVERY LAST ONE OF THEM DETERMINED TO DESTROY HIM. ONLY HIS LOYAL SIDEKICK, THE MIGHTY ECHO, REMAINED BY HIS SIDE AS THE CLIFF CRUMBLED BENEATH HIS HYPERSPEED BOOTS.

THE KID CLOSED HIS EYES, SEARCHING, SEARCHING, SEARCHING FOR A KERNEL OF POWER. SOMETHING, ANYTHING TO HELP DEFEAT THEM.

"The Kid will never crack. Never falter," I told Echo. "I finally know what my superpower is. Silence."

When I noticed I was smothering the Kid with musical notes from the evil spy's trumpet, I scribbled them out, leaving nothing but a big black smudge.

156

SUPERPOWER

I finished painting a blue lightning bolt on the white background of my go-cart the next morning. A clump of Echo's hair floated through the air, sticking to the area over the front left wheel. The creak of a gate and racing footsteps interrupted the quiet summer day. I turned, crouching low, half-expecting to see all of Harmony's ghosts thundering over the alley, but it was only Aidan.

"Look at this, C-C-Cory!"

"A note from Jackson?"

Aidan's eyes narrowed. "Leave h-h-him out of this. D-D-Don't even mention his name to me."

I took the unopened envelope. "What is it?"

Aidan snatched the envelope from my fingers and turned it over. "Look who it's addressed to, C-C-Cory," he said, creasing it with three jabs of his finger.

"Herman Birkbiegler?" I read out loud. "Who the heck is Herman Birkbiegler?"

"Look c-c-closer."

157

I read the address once. Twice. "Anne's house," I whispered.

"Exactly. It was d-d-delivered to us by mistake. D-D-Don't you get it? You were right all along. Anne's real last name isn't Burke. It's B-B-*Birkbiegler*, which can only mean one thing. Her family moved to Harmony to be part of Ziegler's Nazi spy ring."

I leaned back against the workbench and stared at the name on the envelope. Birkbiegler. German through and through.

But then, so was Kuhljuergen. *They can never know.*

"Anya," I said without thinking.

"What?"

"Her real name. It's Anya. That's what she said on the day we first met her. Remember? It's what her grandmother called her, too."

"Anya Katerina Birkbiegler, to be exact."

Aidan and I jerked as if we'd just heard the rat-a-tat-tat of machine gun fire on Satan's Sidewalk. Anne stood there, slingshot dangling at her side. Quick as the Mighty Echo batting at a mouse, she loaded the slingshot with a rock and let it fly. The rock smacked the envelope out of Aidan's hand. It landed on the floor near Aidan's shoe.

"Sawyer wondered why you kept st-st-standing up for Ziegler," Aidan said through clenched teeth. "Now we know. You're one of *them*."

Anne stepped into the shadows of the garage. "We're not Nazis any more than you are, but no one will believe us. It's why my dad lost his store in Joliet and it's why my mother died. The druggist wouldn't sell her the medicine she needed. All because people didn't like the sound of our last name. But we're Americans just like you, Aidan. We're the *good* guys." With each word, Anne's voice grew louder and stronger until she was shouting.

"There's n-n-no such thing as a good German," Aidan snapped. "Tell her, Cory."

Anne turned to me, her blue eyes a mix of anger and hope. She had stood by me after Dad died. Helping me with my go-cart. She hadn't expected anything from me at all. Until now.

Dad's silver dollar sat heavy in my pocket. Two days earlier, I would've stood side by side with my best friend. But now I had my own secret. A secret that tumbled all my words and thoughts into one giant cannonball of confusion.

"C-C-Cory?" Aidan stammered. "Say s-s-something."

It wasn't the Kid's *X* of impenetrable glue over my lips that kept me silent. Anne had been right all along. I *had* jumped to a conclusion about Ziegler based on nothing but pure hatred. If I admitted that to Aidan, he'd think I was siding with Anne instead of him and I'd lose my best friend forever. Was the truth worth that?

I stared down at the letter, knowing that everything balanced on this tick-tock of time. I'd never be able to take back whatever I did or said. Not in a million years.

Anne stooped, retrieved the letter by Aidan's foot, then

stood up and matched his stare nose-to-nose. "I don't blame you for being embarrassed, Aidan," she said, her voice sounding like one of Echo's hisses. "Because after you bragged all summer about how your brother was going to defeat the Nazis single-handedly, he ran away."

"Nobody talks about my br-br-brother that way. Especially a *German*." And then Aidan surprised us both with a sucker punch to Anne's jaw.

Anne's head snapped back and she fell, landing on the seat of her overalls. She didn't stay down. She pushed off the ground and rushed Aidan, head-butting him in the gut.

My comic book fell out of my pocket when I jumped out of the way.

Aidan slipped on it, tearing the cover halfway off, and fell sideways right where Echo hunkered. Echo hissed and slashed his arm, leaving three lines of blood.

Aidan swung blind, connecting with Echo's haunches, flinging him halfway across the garage. Echo scrambled for balance and raced out the door just as Anne planted an elbow in Aidan's stomach. The air left him with a big whoosh, but he shoved her away and scrambled up, blocking the door. His hands clenched in white-knuckled fists.

Anne wasn't backing down. Not one bit. She clawed up the workbench to face him.

Aidan glanced my way. There was a look of pure hatred there, and I could tell he had crossed some invisible line where he couldn't be stopped. "This is your chance to b-b-be a hero, Cory. Help me p-p-pound this Nazi into the ground."

Aidan stepped toward Anne, eyeing the center of her face. His foot landed right on top of my comic book. He paused just long enough to kick it out of the way. The Space Warrior's icy eyes glared at me from the torn cover.

Birkbiegler.

The Warrior told the truth and fought for what was right. Always.

Kuhljuergen.

The only thing that made me different from Anne was the span of one single generation.

Anne didn't flinch when Aidan lunged. I did. I grabbed Aidan around his stomach and pulled back. Hard.

"L-L-Let. Me. G-G-Go!" he screamed, his voice breaking in raspy breaths. His face was red and streaked with sweat, and blood from his arm smeared both our shirts. "What're you st-st-stopping me for?"

Right then; right there. It was my moment. Was my superpower silence? Or was it truth?

I couldn't do it. Couldn't blow my own cover. I couldn't tell the truth.

"Because we have no proof."

"And you never will," Anne said, "because you're wrong." She reached down and picked up the letter for the second time, then she turned and marched back across Satan's Sidewalk.

Anne was gone, but the fight didn't leave Aidan as he

pushed me away. "All this t-t-time, you've bragged about how br-br-brave you are, acting all high-and-mighty just because the t-t-town put up a statue of your g-g-grandfather before you were even b b born. Because your dad enlisted and mine and Sawyer's didn't. But when it came time to face the enemy, *I* was the one that came up f-f-fighting and *you* chickened out. Sawyer is right. You're nothing but a ch-ch-chicken shit!"

Mom had said it took a different kind of courage to tell the truth, and when it came to tossing that coin of courage I had blown it. But I couldn't admit that. Not to Aidan. Not now. I had to smooth things over, say something to save our friendship. "It wasn't a fair fight, and you know it."

"Fair?" Aidan asked. "What is it you're always sp-sp-spouting from the Space Warrior? '*Nothing* is f-f-fair when it comes to evil.'"

"This is different," I said. "You can't beat up on a girl. Especially Anne."

"*She* isn't your friend, Cory. You said so last night." Aidan stepped into the alley before turning one last time. "But I am. You better remember who your *real* fr-fr-friends are. B-B-Before it's too late."

162

REVENGE

One day stretched into another. A week dragged by after Jackson left for Oregon. A week since we'd learned about Anne. Or Anya. And a week since Mom had told me about my great-grandparents. A week since I'd turned my back on the truth.

I spent time yanking weeds out of Mom's Victory Garden and suffering through at least a dozen odd jobs for Mrs. Springgate. Sawyer was probably splitting a gut seeing me doing what he called "girly work." Maybe he wouldn't be so quick to make fun if he did a lick of work himself and saw it wasn't so easy-peasy.

Sometimes Aidan and Sawyer played catch in Aidan's yard. Sometimes they holed up in the garage. Most of the time, they sat in the tree house, the one I'd helped Aidan build. They were talking about me, I was sure. Anne and me. Or Anya. Whatever her real name was. But I didn't let it bother me. Much. There wasn't room for three up there anyway so I kept my cap low over my eyes, pretending not to see them and waiting for things to blow over.

"Aidan'll get over it," I told Echo. I'd seen Aidan mad plenty of times before and he always cooled down. Still, I missed my friend. I missed my dad, too. Missed how things used to be. Mom asked about Aidan almost every day, wondering why he wasn't hanging around. I couldn't tell her what had happened. At least I had Echo to talk to. "You shouldn't have ripped open Aidan's arm. He's the only real friend I have."

"Mrr-oww."

"You're more than a friend. You're the Mighty Echo."

I was in the garage, putting the finishing touches on my go-cart, when I heard footsteps on Satan's Sidewalk. Aidan and Sawyer stopped in the door, shoulder-to-shoulder.

"Looks good," Sawyer said, nodding at my paint job. It had dried hard and glossy and looked impenetrable. Like I had to be.

"You still sore at me?" I asked Aidan.

Aidan looked at Sawyer as if he needed permission, then back to me. "N-N-Naw."

"Of course he isn't," Sawyer said. "Not over some little rhubarb about a girl. Even though that girl is *German*. We know you had a reason. After all, love trumps everything, and you're in *love* with her, right?" Then he puckered up and made sloppy kissy-kissy noises.

I felt the blood pumping through my wrists when I clenched my fingers in a fist, but I took a deep breath.

They could never know.

"She's *not* my girlfriend," I said for the bazillionth time, working at making my voice even. "I was only saving Aidan from getting into trouble. His mom would ground him for eternity if she found out he hit a girl, and you both know it."

Sawyer slapped Aidan on the shoulder. "See? I told you Cory's one of us, part of our team."

"Didn't f-f-feel that way," Aidan muttered.

"You're my best friend," I said. "I got your back, just like you have mine. Right?"

Aidan didn't answer, but Sawyer did. "That's right. Which is why we're here. You still want revenge against the Germans, right?"

They could never know.

I slipped my hand into my pocket, wrapped my fingers around Dad's silver dollar, and nodded.

"Thought so," Sawyer said. "We've got a plan to put An-*YA* in her place, once and for all. Are you with us?"

"It's a p-p-perfect chance for a little Nazi revenge, Cory," Aidan added. "For your d-d-dad."

The silver dollar cooled the blood in my fingers.

They. Could. Never. Know.

"Count me in."

And then they were both in the garage. It felt good to have friends again; to be back inside their circle. "You're not too chicken to do it, are you?" Sawyer asked before telling me their idea.

"Remember, I'm a Woodford. There's not a chicken bone in my family."

165

Aidan narrowed his eyes. "Are you saying my heart p-p-pumps chicken blood since Jackson decided not to f-f-fight? That being yellow runs in *my* b-b-blood the way c-c-courage runs in *yours*?"

My best friend had no idea what really ran through my veins, and he never would. "Don't be a horse's butt. I was just saying you can count on me."

"I told you this would work, Aidan," Sawyer said, grinning around his wad of gum. "It's all about revenge."

Then he leaned in and told me his plan. I thought the whole idea was downright stupid, but I couldn't argue, couldn't side with Anne. Not outright. Not ever. Not if I wanted things to go back to the way they had been. I didn't even care if all Sawyer and Aidan talked about was baseball, just as long as we were friends.

The next day I rolled my cart out of the garage. Echo followed, his tail floating in the air like a giant question mark. Sawyer and Aidan were waiting just like they said they'd be. I parked my cart by a row of trash barrels and then, together, we went up to Anne's back door.

I told myself I was the Kid, out to avenge my father's death with my compatriots at my side. My steps, angry and determined, thundered across the land, threatening to uproot trees and crumble entire mountainsides. Even so, there was a ghostly whisper of doubt against my skin and I noticed a little twinge of guilt.

Anne opened the door, not bothering to invite us in. One of her eyes was surrounded by dark purple and there was a scab on her elbow. I was surprised her dad hadn't called all our mothers and gotten our hides tanned for fighting. She definitely didn't look like a prissy girl. Didn't sound like one, either. "What do you want?"

Sawyer spoke for all of us. "Cory said you dared him to a race. Well, today's the day. He's ready to prove that a girl can never beat a boy."

"So you're one of them now?" she asked, her eyes on me.

"Watch it, *Nazi*," Sawyer said.

"I'm NOT a Nazi," she said. "I'm German. There's a difference."

They could never know.

"Are you going to race or not?" I asked. "We have a hill. The perfect hill." Then I turned and pointed down Satan's Sidewalk. "Let's see whose cart is best, once and for all."

"We dare you," Sawyer added.

"Double D-D-DOG dare you," Aidan said.

"You're on," she said. "And I'll beat you. *All* of you."

We waited on Satan's Sidewalk for Anne to roll out her cart from the garage and line up in the space we left for her. She reached over and rubbed one of Echo's ears while taking a long look at the other go-carts. She ran her hand over the crate that formed the driver's cage on my cart, touching the lightning bolt. "Looks good," she said.

I had to give Anne credit. She was trying to be nice, but I knew this truce was as fragile as spider silk. Then she looked at the one Aidan and Sawyer had built. It wasn't much; just an angled plywood base topped with a used sofa cushion.

"What's that for?" she asked, toeing a piece of wood attached at a lazy angle on the side of the base. At the end was what looked like the rubber tip of a walking cane.

I wondered the same thing but Sawyer stopped Aidan from answering. "Quit stalling, Anne. Or should we call you An-*YA*?"

Sawyer draped an arm over my shoulder as if we were best pals. Aidan stepped beside him. We were a force of three. Strong and unwavering.

Anne eyeballed each one of us. When her eyes met mine, they turned cold and hard. "I'm ready if you are, Cory," she said. Then she turned and went to her cart.

Sawyer thumped my shoulder. "Cory's ready, aren't you, buddy?"

I nodded. "Let's do this."

Anne's cart was on one side of Satan's Sidewalk, Aidan and Sawyer's on the other. Mine was in the middle.

"Aidan and I flipped a coin," Sawyer said as he dragged the heel of his shoe through the broken gravel to create a starting line. "I'll watch him beat you from the sidelines. Everyone ready?"

As we lined up our carts, making sure the wheels were on the line, Sawyer leaned over and whispered to Aidan. Aidan gave a jerky nod before Sawyer stepped off to the side.

I flexed my fingers and then grasped the sides of my cart. Echo wandered over to where I stood ready to push off. He paused by my ankles and meowed as if asking a question.

"Looks like your cat wants to go for a ride," Sawyer said.

The Mighty Echo. My sidekick. Always at my side. I scooped him up and put him in the foot of the crate.

"On your marks," Sawyer yelled.

The Kid was ready. I pushed my cap down tight on my head and then swung one leg inside the freshly painted armored shell of the Kid's tank. It was impenetrable, like me.

"Get set," Sawyer said.

The Kid's muscles were springs the size of tree trunks, his arms chiseled rock.

"Go!"

I pushed off, swinging my other leg inside the crate and ducking low as I picked up speed. Faster than ghosts or Nazis or any other villain attempting to thwart me. Faster and faster, I barreled down Satan's Sidewalk.

I. Would. Not. Be. Beaten.

Echo scrambled around by my shoes, bouncing from the rough ride. This was no place for Echo. Too late now. I couldn't stop.

Rushing air billowed my shirtsleeves. My teeth rattled and the steering rope dug into my hands. I imagined the air currents parting around the Kid's Helmet of Power until my baseball cap caught a gust of wind and flew off my head.

Echo finally stopped scrambling and huddled between my knees. The Mighty Echo was giving in to the ride of his life.

We were neck-and-neck. All three carts bouncing over rocks and broken gravel. Anne pulled ahead. She had been right. The crate on my cart created drag. Out of the corner of my eye, I saw Aidan look my way, checking to see if I would follow the plan.

It was now or never.

I jerked the left rope and the axle turned. My go-cart swerved, shaving off a sliver of paint as it sideswiped Anne's cart.

"Watch out!" she screamed, struggling for control.

Make sure Aidan wins. That was the plan. My part was to keep Anne from taking the lead. Even if it meant crashing into her.

Her go-cart bounced, but she was able to right it and keep going. Sawyer ran behind us, whooping like it was the end of the world. Anne screaming, Sawyer yelling, the carts bouncing: Ziegler's hounds howled at all of it.

"Now!" Sawyer screamed from behind us.

I saw Aidan grab the stick on the side of his cart and pull hard so that the rubber-tipped end dug into loose rock. He threw his feet over each side, his heels trenching Satan's Sidewalk. His cart spewed gravel and fishtailed all the way around before swerving off the pavement and crashing into a trash barrel.

My cart surged ahead. What was he doing? He was supposed to win, not me.

At that exact moment, I was aware of things that made no difference to life and death whatsoever. I smelled rotten potato peelings. I heard the crunch of wheels. I felt the heat of Echo clinging against my legs for all he was worth.

And then, too late, I realized I'd let Aidan and Sawyer get me so riled up about making sure Anne lost that I had forgotten to think about one important thing. I had no way to stop.

23

ENEMY TERRITORY

Anne straddled the baseboard of her cart, digging her Keds into the gravel and sending her cart tail-spinning right. Me? I couldn't get my feet over the high walls of the crate, so I ducked, curling my body over Echo to protect him as best I could. It's what the Space Warrior would have done.

My body bounced to the right, then jerked left when I collided with Ziegler's gate. Wood splintered and my go-cart careened into his backyard, smashing into a tree root that tripped the front axle and snapped it in half. The cart lurched forward, nose-diving into the ground. It buckled, rolled, cracked, and split apart, dumping me out onto the packed dirt and tearing Echo from my arms. Go-cart pieces scattered around me like a giant box of pick-up sticks.

Echo grunted. He landed ten feet in front of me, ears back and tail lashing. Putting him in the cart was the dumbest thing I'd ever done, second only to racing down Satan's Sidewalk in the first place. That, and trusting Sawyer.

I crawled toward Echo, afraid he was hurt, but something stopped me cold.

Snarling.

I looked to my right, to the left.

Nothing.

Sweat rolled down my forehead, dripped off my nose, and pinpricked my leg. I turned my head just enough to see behind me. What I saw gripped my chest until I couldn't breathe.

Ziegler's two wolfhounds stood so close I could have spit on them if I'd had enough saliva in my mouth. I didn't. Their heads were lowered, lips curled to show teeth that were white at the tips, yellow in the middle, and black at the gums. The fangs glistened with slobber.

I heard scrambling in the alley, followed by running, but I didn't look. My eyes stayed glued on the dogs. I didn't have a drop of spit left to swallow, but my throat tried anyway. Every muscle and nerve tensed waiting for the attack, wanting to run, expecting to die.

Aidan and Sawyer's voices came from above the trees, and I realized they must've run into the Mallory house to get a birds-eye view.

"Where are all your superpowers now?"

"And your Woodford Br-Br-Bravery?"

If I tried to escape, the dogs would catch me in less than two steps. Maybe faster. I willed myself to sit still, but the thought of running made my legs twitch. It was just a tiny shudder but those dogs saw it. They growled and barked all at once. I felt the heat from their bodies and prepared to be torn apart. My legs jerked and a scream raked my throat.

Thwok!

Thwok!

Two stones flew across the yard and made contact with the rumps of each giant dog. One of them yelped. I wasn't sure if it was Odin or Pandora. They both took their eyes off me to face this new attacker.

I dared to look away. Aidan and Sawyer were exactly where I thought, hanging out of the Mallorys' second-floor window. But Anne had sneaked into Ziegler's yard and angled her way along the fence to get a good shot at the hounds with her slingshot. "Run, Cory," she said. She tried to keep her voice low, but I heard the panic. "*Run.*"

I lunged, grabbed Echo, and bolted for the opening in the fence just as the hounds went for Anne, blocking her escape route. She scrambled up the maple, clinging to a branch above the dogs as they reared up and placed giant paws on the trunk, their jaws mere inches from the seat of her pants.

Echo dug his claws into my shoulders, but I didn't let him go. The Kid would never abandon the Mighty Echo. I hauled myself up to the second floor of the old Mallory house so fast I didn't have time to worry about ghosts or rotten floorboards.

"I thought you were my friend," I said as I shoved Aidan

aside and searched below for Anne. She had scrambled to a higher branch.

"You think your f-f-family name is better than ours just b-b-because our dads couldn't enlist like yours. B-B-But we just proved you're nothing but a chicken, Cory."

I couldn't believe those words were coming out of my best friend's mouth. I had never bragged. It was just common knowledge that I had to follow in my grandfather's footsteps. "You fathead," I snapped. "Did you do this because of *Jackson*?"

Aidan shoved me so hard I dropped Echo. "Leave J-J-Jackson out of this."

The truth hit me like a German war tank. Sawyer had said this was all about revenge. They had been out for revenge, all right. Only it wasn't against Germans or Anne. Aidan was getting back at me for stopping him from beating the snot out of Anne. They set me up, turning me into bait for a Nazi spy and his dogs. I had escaped, thanks to Anne. Now those dogs circled the tree, snapping at her Keds. Anne tried to climb higher in the tree but her hand slipped, and she nearly fell.

"We have to help her," I said.

"No. We don't," Sawyer told me. "All summer long, you've been bragging about saving Harmony from the Germans. Now it's time to play hardball and put your money where your mouth is. Let her fall, Cory. Let the dogs tear An-*YA* apart."

Aidan nodded. "Time to ch-ch-choose, Cory. Us? Or *her*?"

I didn't want to believe they would actually let Anne get hurt, but their words, so cold and full of hate, hit me in the gut. I suddenly thought of the radio reports describing what the Nazis were doing to Jews and anyone else Hitler hated. Rounding them up and shipping them off to camps in cattle cars. Killing millions without even knowing them. Without knowing the people who were moms and dads and teachers and nurses. Or managers in hardware stores.

Aidan had been my best friend for as long as I could remember, but it was Anne who had helped me build my go-cart. She was the one who had been there, day in and day out, after Dad died. And it was Anne who had come back to help Echo and me when Aidan had run.

Mom had been right. Hate was a very dangerous thing.

"You were right about one thing, Sawyer," I said. "Actions *do* speak louder than words. That's how I know Anne is no more a Nazi than I am."

"Of course you're not. You won't let us forget that your last name is Woodford. But her last name is *Birkbiegler*." Sawyer said. "German. Just like Ziegler."

This was a real-life truth-or-dare moment. Keeping my mouth shut would save me, save the Woodford name. But the truth was so powerful that it bubbled up and broke through my impenetrable seal of silence. "You've known me all my life, Aidan. You know I'm American through and through, right?"

"Yeah. S-S-So what?"

"My great-grandmother's last name was *Kuhljuergen*."

"You mean you're one of *them*?" Sawyer sputtered.

This game of truth-or-dare had turned deadly real. I stared Sawyer straight in the eyes. "What are you going to do about it? Throw *me* to the hounds, too?"

My sidekick, the Mighty Echo, backed me up. "Mrr-oww?"

I kept my eyes on Sawyer, but I should've been watching Aidan, because he was the one who grabbed the scruff of Echo's neck. I reached for my cat, but Aidan took a giant step back. Echo hissed, his paws scratching at thin air. "We c-c-can't throw you, Cory, but we can throw your stupid c-c-cat."

And then my best friend dangled Echo out the broken window.

"Aidan, don't! You wouldn't *dare*."

"He's daring you, Aidan. Do it. I double *dog* dare you," Sawyer said with a snort. And then he shoved Aidan. It was just a little push, not really meant to do any harm, but it was enough to throw Aidan off balance. Enough to make him let go of Echo.

"*No!*" I screamed. For one horrifying moment my cat twisted through the air before his fall was broken by the tangled branches surrounding Ziegler's yard. He bounced, slid, and then hit the ground so hard he yowled with pain. He hunkered in Ziegler's yard, one leg cocked at an angle. The Mighty Echo was trapped dead center in enemy territory, and he was hurt. Bad.

24

THE TRUE ADVENTURES OF THE WARRIOR KID

Pandora and Odin circled Echo, their lips curled up in growling grins.

No time to think.

No time to argue.

Sawyer said something about Echo being a worthless stray. Aidan stammered, his words totally stuck inside his suddenly white face.

No time to listen.

No time to fight.

I flew down the steps, willing my feet to be as fast as the Kid's HyperSpeed Boots.

No time. No time. No time.

A step gave way. I pulled free, splinters clawing into my leg.

No time. No time. No time.

Past all the Mallory ghosts. Past the ghosts of Dad and Grandpa. Scattering them all.

No time. No time. No time.

Through the Mallorys' overgrown yard. Around the tight corner to the alley. Straight to what was left of the

Demons' Door.

I stopped then, heart pounding, blinking away the blur in my eyes.

The sun glinted off something lying in the middle of Ziegler's yard. Dad's silver dollar mocked me from a puddle of sun. I was supposed to be a hero like my grandfather and dad, but I had no Helmet of Power or HyperSpeed Boots and this was no comic book. It was real. I was nothing but a scrawny eleven-year-old kid and I was scared spitless.

I stepped into Ziegler's yard anyway.

"They're going to tear Echo to pieces," Anne screamed, stripping bark as she slid down the tree. One of the beasts turned and eyed Anne, stopping her cold.

Echo backed against the fence, one leg useless. He couldn't run. He had nowhere to go even if could. He faced the hounds, ears back and hackles up.

"Help!" Anne screamed. "Somebody help!"

Nobody else was there. No one but me.

There was fear in Echo's eyes, but beneath it I saw something else. Trust. I couldn't turn back. I wouldn't.

Sweat stung my eyes. There were no superpowers bubbling through my veins, but I sucked in air, searching for a pebble of strength from deep within. Memories exploded like hand grenades. Mr. Ziegler walking through the park; his warning that the dogs would bite. But he had said something else, too. Odin and Pandora were trained. Trained to obey.

I couldn't afford a quiver. Not now. I willed my voice to

be firm, loud, and as low as my toenails. "Odin. Pandora. Come here. Come!"

"No," Anne yelled. "They'll kill you!"

Their ears flicked and Pandora swiveled her massive head to eyeball me for a split second before turning back to Echo.

Ziegler had said his dogs obeyed. Why hadn't they moved? My mind tumbled over memories of Ziegler commanding his dogs to come. To be quiet. To stay.

I realized what I had done wrong. Knew, then, what I had to do.

"Odin. Pandora," I said again. I pushed my voice past my pounding heart and said the worst thing possible. "*Komm! Fuß!*"

My knees threatened to buckle as both dogs' massive heads swiveled this time. Their eyes latched onto mine. I fought the urge to run, willing the courage of every comic book hero in the history of mankind into my voice. "*Komm!*"

Odin snapped up the slobber dripping from his mouth, torn between Echo and me.

"*Fuß.*"

The giant dog huffed, locked eyes with me, and took a step. I looked into his eyes. "*Fuß.*"

Odin took another step, then picked up speed. I wanted to run. To scream. To fly away. But I planted my feet as Odin headed straight for me. "*Komm!*" I repeated, a touch of panic making my voice go up.

The dog was huge, his black nose even with mine. He tasted the air in front of my face, the hair surrounding his muzzle matted with slobber. He grunted, smacked his lips again. Then he turned and found his place at my left side.

Pandora had watched. I met her gaze, snapped my fingers. "Pandora. *Fuß!*"

And this time, she did.

Their fangs were inches from my jugular, and their breath panted hot in my face. Gray hair stuck to my sweat-soaked arms as I reached out and curled shaking fingers around the dogs' collars. "*Sitz!*"

I heard Sawyer using words that would get him grounded for a year, but I didn't look up. I kept my eyes on Echo. So did Pandora and Odin. Their bodies quivered at the sound of Anne scrambling down the tree. Her Keds slapped broken gravel as she fled, leaving me standing one inch away from the jaws of death.

"Stay," I repeated. "*Bleib!*"

"Your girlfriend left you high and dry. You know that, don't you?" Sawyer yelled.

Aidan had been my best friend, but now he sounded just like Sawyer. "You can't stay there f-f-forever."

I would not let go. No. Matter. What.

Pandora growled when Echo tried to scoot farther back into the thicket of weeds growing up around the bushes. "Don't move," I reminded her. I tried to mimic the syllables I'd heard Ziegler used to make his dogs come and sit and stay. I hoped I got them close enough. "*Bleib!*"

I stood there for so long I expected snowflakes to start falling. My legs stiffened and my fingers tingled from the loss of blood. Odin whined. Pandora smacked her lips. Still, I held on.

The back door broke the spell, opening so fast it crashed against a wall. "*Was ist passiert?*" a thick voice asked.

I finally broke away from Echo's eyes and slowly turned my head. There, standing in the door, stood Ziegler. He wore pajamas and his hair was ruffled. It didn't occur to me until that second that he might be sleeping during the day, though it made sense since he worked nights at the VFW.

Next to him was Anne. She hadn't left me stranded at all. She must have gone for help, running to the front of Ziegler's house, pounding on windows and doors to wake him. Anne was the one who did what it took to save me from being torn to shreds. Not Aidan. And definitely not Sawyer.

Mr. Ziegler surveyed the yard. The broken gate. My splintered go-cart. He spotted Sawyer and Aidan just before they ducked back in the window. "Get down from there," he yelled. "Before the floor cavez in and zwallows you whole."

Anne pushed past him, taking one step toward Echo before Odin's growl stopped her cold.

I. Did. Not. Let. Go.

Mr. Ziegler placed a hand on Anne's shoulder to hold her still, and eyeballed Odin. "Behave, you big brute."

There wasn't a hint of fear in his voice. His sleep-swollen eyes swept across the yard to land on Echo hunkering in the corner. His eyes widened as he put the pieces together. I waited for him to yell. To accuse us of spying. To threaten us. Instead he came down the steps and asked, "Itz anyone hurt? Besides the cat?"

I didn't want to make a sound, afraid the dogs might turn and sink their teeth into my throat if I did. So I gave a little shake of my head.

Mr. Ziegler came across the yard then. Walking slowly. Calmly. The man I had accused of being my enemy reached out and gently put his hands over mine, slipping his fingers beneath the collars. "You can let go now, Cory," he said. "I have them. You did good. You are a brave boy. A very brave boy."

The two giant dogs slipped away from me to follow Mr. Ziegler into the house. My knees were like jelly, but I couldn't sit down. Not yet. I made my way across the yard and squatted in front of Echo. His eyes were wild and he growled. "It's okay," I soothed.

Mr. Ziegler came back outside carrying a towel. My cat was too surprised to move when Mr. Ziegler gently but firmly wrapped the towel around him and lifted him from the ground. "We vill take him to Dr. Simon. You and me," Mr. Ziegler said.

I finally found my voice. "We can't afford a veterinarian. Not since Dad . . ."

"Don't you worry," Mr. Ziegler said. "This one needz our help and I vill help. After all, that iz what neighbors do. As soon as I am ready we vill go."

I met Mr. Ziegler's gaze when he placed Echo in the cradle of my arms. I'd never seen him up close. His eyes weren't shifty or mean; not a spy's eyes at all. They were worried and kind. The way one friend looks at another to let them know they care.

How could I ever have thought Mr. Ziegler was some crazed Nazi trying to take over Harmony? He was just a man with a funny accent who loved music and wanted to be a good neighbor. Like Anne, or even old Mrs. Springgate. They had each proved it over and over, only I was too busy trying to be a hero to notice.

Echo lay limp in my arms, tiny tremors vibrating his body with each breath. With the fight drained from him, he looked small and scared, nothing like a superhero's sidekick from one of my comic books. Still, he had been brave when he needed to be. "It's okay, Echo," I said again. "I've got you, now. Mr. Ziegler's going to help us."

Those words seemed to hang in the air. The man I'd plotted against all summer long was now the very person I was counting on to help make everything okay again.

I glanced at my splintered go-cart. At the gate I'd crashed through. Up at the empty window of the haunted house. Finally, I looked over at Anne standing right next to me.

"I'm sorry, Anne," I said. "This is my fault. All of it. I was wrong, and I was wrong to say all those things about you, too. I made a mess out of everything. If you never talk to me again, I'll understand."

I wouldn't have blamed Anne if she had turned and stomped away, but she didn't.

The sun glinted off Dad's silver dollar lying in the dust and Anne picked it up. I cradled Echo in one arm so I could take it from her, turning it over to see how both sides were worn so smooth they looked the same. "Truth or dare?" I asked Anne. "Were you scared?"

Anne grinned so big the constellations of freckles on her cheeks squished together. "Truth is easy. I was so scared I nearly wet my pants!"

"Me, too," I admitted.

"That makes what you did even braver," she said. "You really are Woodford Brave."

The door opened and Mr. Ziegler hurried outside. He was ready to go. Ready to help Echo. To help me.

"I'll go get your ball cap," Anne said.

I glanced up at the Mallory windows. The ghosts were gone, and so were Aidan and Sawyer. Aidan had said I had to choose. Him or Anne. I flipped Dad's silver dollar and watched it somersault through the air. But when it slapped back into my palm, I slipped it into my pocket without bothering to look at it.

"It's okay," I told her. "I don't need my cap now."

Then I reached out and took Anne's hand. Together, we followed Mr. Ziegler through the splintered remains of what used to be the Demons' Door.

AUTHOR'S NOTE

World War II was not the war of my youth. Vietnam was.

Vietnam was not a popular war by the time my brother Randy turned eighteen and was eligible for the draft. Vivid television reports about Agent Orange and the Vietcong intermingled with antiwar demonstrations and sit-ins. Some, like the one on the campus of Kent State, erupted in life-ending violence. I remember my family anxiously waiting to learn Randy's draft number. Everything depended on that one number. My brother's number was high, which meant he wouldn't be called to enlist right away. A neighbor, however, was not so lucky.

One night my neighbor packed a few things, got in his car, and headed for the Canadian border. While some called draft dodgers "cowards," I couldn't help but imagine what it must have been like to leave family, friends, and the only home he'd known in the dead of night and drive blindly to a foreign country. That sounded pretty brave to me—a different kind of bravery. Thus the seed for *Woodford Brave* was planted.

When recent conflicts erupted in the Middle East, I found myself examining my own beliefs. It occurred to me that while the languages of our country's enemies may change, the central themes of conflict, bravery, and prejudice during times of war do not. I tested my "ah-ha" moment by reading about the war of my parents' youth—World War II. And that's where I found Cory's story.

Cory and his world are made up, but as so often happens, a writer's real life creeps into the writing. Jackson, of course, is reminiscent of my childhood neighbor who showed me a different side of courage. The idea for Ziegler's dogs came from the two Irish wolfhounds that terrorized my walks to and from elementary school each and every day. And, yes, their gate was much too small and feeble to contain them.

What about the silver dollar that Cory's dad carried in his pocket? If you look on my desk, you will find the silver dollar my own father carried in his pocket every single day from as far back as I could remember until the day he died. The rim and both sides are worn smooth from his worrying it.

I found most of my information about life in the 1940s from books and online research. My best source, however, was my mother, who sat in her den and reminisced about being a young telephone operator when the war broke out. She told me how the switchboard lit up the day war was declared. How the telephone operators knew that something big had happened. They just had no idea *how* big. She told me about the boys who rushed to enlist and how everyday items like silk stockings and gasoline became scarce due to rationing. Mom told me the story about my Uncle Arnold who came home on leave after the Battle of Midway and spoke at a Main Street rally encouraging everyone to support the war effort by buying war bonds.

My mother also told me about meeting a sailor named Robert Thornton who was home on leave because his ship had been torpedoed. A handsome man with deep-brown eyes who once played a trumpet in nightclubs. By the end of the evening, Mom had exchanged addresses with the sailor, and after he went back to his Navy ship they started writing to each other.

So while my father was off fighting a war started by the Nazis, he was falling in love with a girl. A girl named Thelma. Thelma Kuhljuergen. A girl whose veins pumped German blood.

The author's dad's silver dollar
(photograph courtesy of William Andersen)

BOOKS

Adams, Simon. *DK Eyewitness Books: World War II*. New York: DK Publishing, 2007.

Ambrose, Stephen E. *The Good Fight: How World War II Was Won*. New York: Atheneum Books for Young Readers, 2001.

Brokaw, Tom. *The Greatest Generation*. New York: Random House, 2001.

Cohen, Stan. *V For Victory: America's Home Front During World War II*. Missoula, MT: Pictorial Histories Publishing, 1991.

Colman, Penny. *Rosie the Riveter: Women Working on the Home Front in World War II*. New York: Crown Books for Young Readers, 1998.

Easley, MaryAnn. *Knuckle Down*. BookSurge Publishing, 2009.

Grun, Bernard. *The Timetables of History: A Horizontal Linkage of People and Events*. New York: Simon & Schuster, 1963.

Homes, Richard, et al. *World War II: The Definitive Visual History*. New York: DK Adult, 2011.

Josephson, Judith Pinkerton. *Growing Up in World War II: 1941 to 1945*. Minneapolis: Lerner Publishing Group, 2003.

Macy, Sue. *A Whole New Ball Game: The Story of the All-American Girls Professional Baseball League*. New York: Puffin, 1995.

Maslon, Laurence, and Michael Kantor. *Superheroes!: Capes,*

Cowls, and the Creation of Comic Book Culture. New York: Crown
Archetype, 2013.

Mazer, Harry. *A Boy at War: A Novel of Pearl Harbor.* New York:
Simon & Schuster Books for Young Readers, 2012.

Osborne, Mary Pope. *My Secret War: The World War II Diary of
Madeline Beck.* New York: Scholastic, 2000.

Peck, Richard. *On the Wings of Heroes.* New York: Dial, 2007.

Reynolds, Clark G. *America at War: 1941–1945, the Home Front.*
New York: Gallery Books, 1990.

Tripp, Valerie. *Meet Molly, An American Girl: 1944.* Middleton, WI:
Pleasant Company, 1986.

Uschan, Michael V. *A Cultural History of the United States Through the
Decades: The 1940s.* San Diego: Lucent Books, 1998.

WEBSITES*

Ardman, Harvey. "World War II: German Saboteurs Invade
America in 1942." Weider History: HistoryNet.com. http://
www.historynet.com/world-war-ii-german-saboteurs-invade-
america-in-1942.htm.

"August 8, 1942: German saboteurs executed in Washington."
This Day In History. *History Channel* website. http://www.
history.com/this-day-in-history/german-saboteurs-executed-
in-washington.

"Captain America," "The Golden Age of Bucky," "Bucky (Fred
Davis)," "Bucky (1950s)," "Captain America (1950s),"
"Human Torch," "Young Allies." An International Catalogue
of Superheroes. http://www.internationalhero.co.uk/.

"Comics Checklists." The Big Comic Book DataBase. http://www.
comics-db.com.

Websites active at time of publication.

"George John Dasch and the Nazi Saboteurs." The Federal Bureau of Investigation. http://www.fbi.gov/about-us/history/famous-cases/nazi-saboteurs.

"The Golden Era . . . June 1938 to 1945." ComicBookWebsites. com. http://www.dereksantos.com.

"The Good War and Those Who Refused to Fight It." PBS. http://www.pbs.org/itvs/thegoodwar/.

"The Greatest Amateur Racing Event in the World!" All-American Soap Box Derby. http://www.aasbd.org/.

"League History." Official Website of the All-American Girls Professional Baseball League Players Association. http://www.aagpbl.org/index.cfm/pages/league/12/league-history.

"Making Do With Less: Shortages and Conservation." Life on the Home Front: Oregon Responds to World War II. Oregon State Archives. http://arcweb.sos.state.or.us/pages/exhibits/ww2/services/conserve.htm.

Polsson, Ken. "Chronology of World War II." http://ww2timeline. info/.

Sterner, C. Douglas. "The War Mother's Flag." Home of the Heroes. http://www.homeofheroes.com/hallofheroes/1st_floor/flag/1bfb_disp9b.html.

Thomas, Pauline Weston. "Rationing and Utility Clothing of the 1940s: Fashion History 1940s." Fashion-Era. http://www.fashion-era.com/utility_clothing.htm.

"What if? The Golden Age." Marvel Masterworks Resource Page. http://www.marvelessentials.com.

"World War II Rationing." Online Highways LLC. http://www.u-s-history.com.

"World War II Rationing on the U.S. Homefront." Ames Historical Society. http://www.ameshistory.org/exhibits/events/rationing.htm.

"World War II On The Radio." OTRCAT.com. Old Time Radio Catalog. http://www.otrcat.com/wwii-on-the-radio.html.